Y - L - E

"I know how it is with men,"

Lori said. "Sometimes they mean well, but they never get around to calling. I don't want you to think you're obligated to me."

"Don't you?" Jason paused. "I was hoping you'd be desolate if I didn't keep in touch."

"I'd be more than mildly disappointed." Lori spoke quietly as she smiled up at Jason.

He spoke more softly. "I don't suppose you'd like me to kiss you goodbye?"

His lips descended in what seemed like slow motion. The feather-light brushing of his mouth on hers was no more than a sweet promise of things to come.

Lori knew she was acting foolishly, but she also knew that if Jason picked her up in his arms and carried her off she wouldn't do a single thing to dissuade him....

Dear Reader,

Welcome to Silhouette—experience the magic of the wonderful world where two people fall in love. Meet heroines that will make you cheer for their happiness, and heroes (be they the boy next door or a handsome, mysterious stranger) who will win your heart. Silhouette Romance reflects the magic of love—sweeping you away with books that will make you laugh and cry, heartwarming, poignant stories that will move you time and time again.

In the coming months we're publishing romances by many of your all-time favorites, such as Diana Palmer, Brittany Young, Sondra Stanford and Annette Broadrick. Your response to these authors and our other Silhouette Romance authors has served as a touchstone for us, and we're pleased to bring you more books with Silhouette's distinctive medley of charm, wit and—above all—*romance*.

I hope you enjoy this book and the many stories to come. Experience the magic!

Sincerely,

Tara Hughes
Senior Editor
Silhouette Books

VAL WHISENAND

Treasure Hunters

Silhouette Romance

Published by Silhouette Books New York

America's Publisher of Contemporary Romance

SILHOUETTE BOOKS
300 E. 42nd St., New York, N.Y. 10017

Copyright © 1989 by Val Whisenand

ISBN: 0-373-08655-5

First Silhouette Books printing June 1989

Printed in the U.S.A.

VAL WHISENAND

is an incurable romantic who has been married to her high-school sweetheart since she was seventeen. The mother of two grown children, she lives in a house that she designed and she and her husband built with their own hands. Her varied interests have led her to explore many fascinating occupations and to travel throughout the United States and Canada. Whether her goal is to write another book, learn a foreign language or prevail over tremendous odds to become a winning game-show contestant, her natural tenacity sees to it that she succeeds. Once she makes up her mind, there's no stopping her!

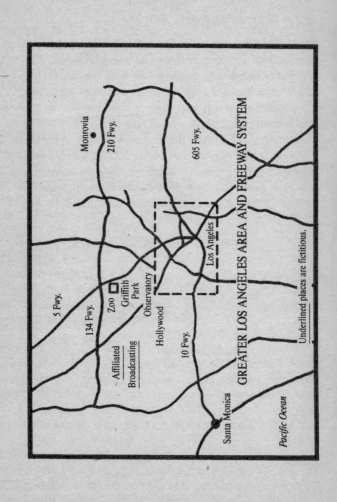

GREATER LOS ANGELES AREA AND FREEWAY SYSTEM

Underlined places are fictitious.

Monrovia

210 Fwy.

605 Fwy.

Los Angeles

5 Fwy.

134 Fwy.

Zoo

Griffith Park

Observatory

Affiliated

Broadcasting

Hollywood

10 Fwy.

Santa Monica

Pacific Ocean

Prologue

Jason Daniels's brown eyes gleamed below his furrowed brow as he ran his fingers through his thick, dark hair. "You've got to be kidding, Brad. Me? A quiz-show contestant? That's ridiculous. I came to *work* in Fair Practices, not to play games." His gaze lingered on the waves gently lapping the shoreline and followed the darting, diving dance of the seabirds overhead.

"I know." Trudging along on the soft sand and doing his best to keep up with his old friend, the stocky young man spread his hands wide in a gesture of futility. "I told them I knew you from when we worked together at WQP in Chicago and I was positive you wouldn't like the idea."

"And?" Jason crammed his hands into the pockets of his slacks.

"No deal," Brad said. "I warned you before you took this job what a stickler for detail old man McAlister is. If he says everybody has to, then everybody damn well better."

"I suppose he has the right, as head of Fair Practices," Jason said, "but I still don't see the rationale."

"He says it's to give all his people a feel for the world of the contestants," Brad told him. "So you'll know what they go through."

Jason straightened. "And I gather I'm also expected to keep track of the operatives on regular duty with the game show?"

Shrugging, Brad nodded. "Might as well."

Jason stopped walking, grabbed Brad's arm and brought him to a halt. "Was that why you insisted on meeting me here on the beach first, instead of taking me to my office?"

"Hey. Ease up. I was just following orders. McAlister doesn't want you to be seen at the studio until after you've completed your little undercover assignment. That's all."

"Terrific." Jason rubbed the back of his neck with one hand. "Okay. Let's hear it. When and where do I start?"

Brad breathed a sigh of relief. "You're supposed to take the rest of this week off. Make like a tourist and enjoy that condo you managed to slip into your contract. The preliminary tryouts are at Sunset Boulevard in Hollywood at 10:00 a.m. on Monday."

He reached into his pocket and handed Jason a slip of paper. "Here. I wrote the address down for you. The contestant coordinator and the producer know you'll be there, so you'll have no problem getting picked for the final contestant pool." He looked up seriously. "No one else is in on the plan."

"What name shall I use?"

"They're expecting Jason Daniels," Brad said. "Since it's not that unusual a name, we figured you'd have an easier time of it if you kept your own identity."

"Thanks loads." Jason opened the top two buttons of his shirt, then undid the cuffs and rolled back his sleeves to bare his forearms before continuing down the beach. "Have you worked up a full background on me or should I take care of those details myself?"

Brad stumbled, recovered and scurried to keep up. "We've left that all up to you. Might as well keep it close to reality so you can avoid slipups."

"And I suppose the old man wants a full report on his field people?"

Smiling, Brad clapped him on the back. "In triplicate. But cheer up. It'll only be for a week or so and then you can come back to your classy new office, start to play the executive again and get the welcome you deserve from your staff."

"Yeah, sure. If any of them are speaking to me by then."

"They will be. Remember, every one of them went through the same ritual at some point." Brad grinned sheepishly. "Even me. It wasn't too bad."

Jason couldn't bring himself to return Brad's smile. He'd cut his old ties in Chicago, moved to Los Angeles and hired on at Affiliated Broadcasting as an assistant to the head of the Fair Practices Department, expecting to spend his days safely sequestered behind a desk making sure that the network's game shows were conducted legitimately. Now all that had changed. Damn, he hated deceit.

Cursing under his breath, Jason crammed the piece of paper with the address deeper into his pocket. At thirty-four, he wasn't about to chuck all he'd fought for and start over working for some local station as an errand boy.

No. He'd comply with McAlister's wishes. He had to. But he didn't have to like it.

Chapter One

Lori Kendall stepped calmly into the elevator behind her frizzy-haired friend, smiled and pushed the worn plastic button. "I still don't know why I had to come along, Annette. This quiz-show mania is your problem, not mine."

"You're my best friend." Annette was fussing with the stray strands of a hairdo that made her look as if she'd been attacked in a dark alley by a deranged beautician. She leaned over, trying to see her reflection in the glass-covered, In Case of Emergency sign. "Who else would tell me the truth?"

"Who else would sacrifice the first day of her vacation to come to downtown Hollywood with you?" Lori added. "I must be crazy."

"You can go to the beach and whistle at lifeguards later. Right now, I need your unbiased opinion of my performance." Annette reached over to adjust the lace collar of Lori's blouse and fluff her friend's thick, brown hair so that it lay neatly over her shoulders. "Just don't look *too* gorgeous, will you? They can only use a few of us, and I'd sure hate to lose out to you."

"You told me to wear this outfit, Annette Cole. If you don't like the way it looks, then why—"

"I do. I do. The pale pink color is great with your fair skin and the gold earrings really bring out the hazel of those damn doe eyes of yours." Annette tried to smile. "I'm just nervous, that's all. Look at the way I'm shaking." In slow motion, her jaw dropped open as she held her hands out in front of her. "Oh, my God! One of my nails is chipped!"

Lori put her arm around the shorter girl's shoulders. "You'll live. Believe me. Now, take it easy, or they'll be carrying you out of here on a stretcher."

She saw the number seven light as the elevator opened onto a luxuriously carpeted hall. On the wall opposite the sliding doors was a large, hand-lettered sign that read Contestants, followed by an arrow that pointed to the left. "Looks like they were expecting us," Lori quipped. "Are you ready?"

Annette's voice quivered with excitement. "No! Not yet. I mean I have to find the rest room and fix my hair, my makeup." Her fingers fluttered to her cheeks.

"Oh, for heaven's sake." Lori hooked her arm through Annette's and led her in the direction of the arrow. "Okay. I'm sure you're not the only hopeful wanting to check her appearance before keeping the appointment. Come on. We'll find out where the bathrooms are and repair whatever ravages your nervous temperament has wrought on your poor face."

"You're a wonderful friend."

"I'm a patsy. But what would I do for excitement without you?" Lori asked. She reached an open door and peeked in. Metal-framed chairs lined three of the beige walls. Over the receptionist's desk was a No Smoking sign, and on the wall behind, an impressive collage of celebrities' photographs and autographs. Two young men, a woman with a small child on her lap and an older man with an aquiline nose and protruding ears looked up from their seats in the metal-framed chairs.

"Come on." Lori tried unsuccessfully to get Annette through the door.

"No. You go. I'll wait here." Giving Lori a shove, Annette stepped back into the relative anonymity of the hallway, leaving Lori to walk into the office alone. Seated behind the receptionist's desk was a darkly exotic woman whose instant smile warmed Lori to the core.

Lori returned the smile. "Hello. We have appointments to try out for the new game show." She glanced at the crumpled newspaper clipping in her hand. "*Treasure Hunters*?"

"You've come to the right place. Come on in and have a seat."

"Actually my friend and I have driven a long way on the freeway and we'd like a chance to freshen up first, if we may."

The woman's face expressed perfect understanding. "Sure, honey." She reached into a drawer, removed a large, silver key ring and held it out to Lori. "Take this, go back past the elevators and follow the hall to your right. You can't miss the ladies' room."

"Thanks." Lori rejoined Annette and handed her the ring. "Here. I don't know how you expect to audition to play any kind of game if you're afraid to ask the way to the rest room."

"I just need a little reassurance that I look my best, that's all. Let me see that ad again?" Holding the key tightly in one hand, Annette tucked her purse under her arm, unfolded the clipping and scanned it as she hurried to keep pace with Lori's long, athletic strides.

Lori heard the elevator doors start to open and grabbed her daydreaming friend just as Annette careened into the broad chest of a man stepping into the hall.

"Aagh!" Annette shrieked, staying on her feet only with Lori's help. Breathless, she yanked herself free of Lori's grasp and glared at the stranger.

He was the first to recover. "I *am* sorry. Are both of you ladies all right?"

The man's voice reminded Lori of royal-blue velvet, its tones blanketing her with a lush warmth and bringing a tingly excitement to the hairs on the back of her neck. Bronzed and intense, the man was staring at her with a lop-sided smile on his face that made the slight cleft in his chin almost disappear. Everything about him appealed to her.

Looking up and smiling, Lori blushed and smoothed her skirt. "Yes, thanks. Are you okay, too?" Any fool could see he was fine, Lori told herself, disturbed at how silly she sounded in asking. Oh, boy, was he fine.

He smiled and nodded.

"Good. My friend is on her way to try out for a game show. We should have watched where we were going. Sorry."

"I see. In that case, we'll probably be seeing each other again. That is, if you're here to play *Treasure Hunters*."

"We are!" Annette announced, nearly jumping up and down. "Isn't it exciting!"

"Yes. Very," he said, observing Lori's reactions. He cocked his head to one side and raised his dark eyebrows. "The whole premise doesn't seem to have made you quite as breathlessly enthusiastic as your friend." He extended his right hand. "My name is Jason Daniels. What's yours?"

"Lori Kendall," she said, shaking his hand. "And this is Annette Cole. It's her party, so to speak. I'm just along for the ride."

"You're not trying out?"

Lori was conscious that her hand was still firmly held in Jason's. Staring into the depths of his compelling eyes she noticed how stifling the surrounding air had suddenly become, how dry her mouth was and how unsteady on her feet

their recent encounter had made her. It took several seconds before she was able to make herself withdraw her hand
from Jason's strong, reassuring grasp. She was enraptured
by the way his eyes glistened, the way his mouth moved
when he spoke and by the tiny smile lines at the corners of
his eyes that crinkled when he gazed at her.

"I . . . Yes, I'm trying out. I don't expect to be chosen, of
course. I really have no interest in being on television."

"You don't like the thought of winning a lot of money?"

She laughed, surprised at how nervous she sounded. "I
didn't say that."

"Then maybe we will see each other again. You never
know which qualities these Hollywood types are looking for,
do you?"

"Oh, *I* do," Annette blurted out. "They like vivacious
personalities and good talkers who dress kind of mod, like
me." She tugged at her tight leather skirt, which stopped
just short of indecency, wriggling to ease it down under the
leather belt slung low on her hips. Her yellow blouse was as
oversize as her skirt was small, and it fell off one shoulder
and draped daringly across her left breast.

A small smile began to curl Jason's mouth and Lori noticed, as they exchanged knowing glances, that he had a
dimple in one of his cheeks.

"In that case, I'd better go home," he said, smoothing his
polo shirt and stuffing his hands into the pockets of his
summer wool slacks. "I'm afraid I may be too conservative."

Lori shook her head. "I wouldn't worry, Mr. Daniels. My
friend has made a career of trying out for quiz shows on TV
and she has yet to be chosen to play."

"Oh, thanks a lot," Annette said with a moan. "Just
what I needed to hear to bolster my confidence."

Patting her on the arm, Lori pulled a face. "If you didn't
think you had a chance, you wouldn't be here, so don't get
upset. We need to be fair to Mr. Daniels, too. You wouldn't

want him to give up and leave because of something you said, would you?''

"That would depend on what I thought his chances might be of beating me out of a chance to play," Annette said honestly. "Less competition means better odds."

"I'm ashamed of you," Lori told her. "Half the fun of winning is doing it fairly against a worthy opponent."

"I'd lots rather have money than glory," Annette said. She jingled the rest room key ring at Jason. "Now, if you'll excuse us, I have some major repairs to make. It's almost ten o'clock and I don't want to create a bad impression by being late for my interview." Catching Lori's arm, she dragged her down the hall.

Lori shrugged and shot Jason an apologetic grin, hoping to glimpse his dimple again, but his smile had faded. Funny, she thought. He was about to participate in an exciting new adventure, yet he looked as if he'd rather be elsewhere. Either that, or she was misreading him and he, like Annette, took the competition far too seriously for his own good.

After what seemed like half an hour Lori herded Annette back toward the waiting room. "You're fine. I swear. I wouldn't say so if I didn't believe it."

"You're sure?" Annette slowed her pace even more.

"Trust me." Lori propelled her friend through the open door with one swift push. The room was so crowded they had no place to sit so she left Annette standing by the entrance, staring, while she returned the key to the receptionist.

Annette hadn't moved when Lori rejoined her. "Close your mouth, Annette," Lori teased. "It's impolite to gape."

"But look at all of them. There must be a hundred people here!"

"More like forty, but who's counting? Besides, I wouldn't worry. They all look nervous." She covered the side of her

mouth with her hand and whispered, "At least you're not
giggling like those three girls over there."

"No, I'm too petrified." Annette began to smile. "Some
of the guys look really interesting, though. I like the con-
struction-worker types and the ones in the flowered shirts
who look like they belong on a blanket at the beach, soaking up rays. Don't you?"

"Belong at the beach, you mean? Definitely." Lori
squeezed herself between Annette and a perky, grandmotherly type in a tailored jacket and ruffled blouse. A quick
glance told her that if there was one thing she and all the rest
of the people jammed into the room had in common, it was
that they had nothing in common.

Jason was also standing, Lori noted. He had staked his
claim to a short section of bare wall between two other
doorways and was leaning there, his arms folded across his
chest. She tried smiling at him and was rewarded by his nod
of recognition.

The dusky-skinned receptionist rose from behind her
desk. "I want to welcome you to Halpern-Oldham Produc-
tions and wish you luck. We'll get started as soon as all of
you have your name tags." She picked up three. "I still need
Lori, Jean and Annette. Are you ladies here?"

Annette swished across the room, her small, quick steps
dictated by the constraints of her skirt, her bangle earrings
swinging wildly. Lori and the grandmotherly type followed. Easing the older woman gently ahead, Lori politely
took the last place in line and smiled at her. "Hi. I guess
you're Jean."

"Yes. Isn't this wonderful? I haven't had this much fun
since my husband ran off with his secretary."

Lori couldn't help giggling as she pinned on her name tag.
"You're kidding, of course?"

"Not in the least."

"Oh, dear."

Jean patted her on the arm. "Not to worry. I'm quite content now, and I have my own life to live. I just decided it was time I reached out and did some of the crazy things that I'd only dreamed about before. So, here I am."

"That is wonderful," Lori said. "I'm here to keep a friend company."

Annette elbowed Lori in the ribs as the room grew quiet. "Shush. Listen."

"My name is Simone," the receptionist said. "I'll be giving you some yellow cards to fill out before you meet Vicki, our contestant coordinator. Be sure to answer all the questions and don't leave any of the lines blank."

Lori completed her card quickly and handed it back to Simone. One other person had finished—Jason Daniels. Lori smiled at him as Simone posed them together for the Polaroid ID photos that went in the upper corner of each card. "I guess we either have uncomplicated lives or we organize our thoughts well." She smiled as the camera flashed.

"Something like that," he said, stepping back.

"What do you suppose happens next?"

"I noticed you had the newspaper clipping advertising for contestants. What did it say?"

She tossed her head, swinging her silky hair in an unconsciously sensual gesture. "Not much. You must have seen the ad, too."

Jason held his breath. He'd have to remember to be more careful or he wouldn't last five minutes with someone as quick-witted as Lori Kendall. "I thought perhaps you had read a different description from the one I saw. You know, from another daily."

"I imagine they're all the same ad. That way everyone would be expecting the same thing when they got here."

"True." Jason leaned back against the wall again. Lori was damned attractive, he thought seriously. Instead of a flamboyant outfit like the one her friend was wearing, she was dressed in a simple, lacy blouse and dark skirt, and

adorned with delicately filigreed, understated gold jewelry.
Not only was she the most physically appealing woman in
the room, she was obviously a lady.

"I was talking to Simone before you got here," Jason
said, forcing his mind to stop its flights of fancy, "and she
told me we were in for a long session. Maybe all day."

"All day?" Lori grimaced. "I was kind of hoping I'd get
to the beach later this afternoon." She sighed. "Oh, well.
Annette needs me. I guess I'll live."

Jason's eyes were slightly closed and he'd stuffed his
hands in his pockets. "What does she expect you to do?"

"Critique her. I'm supposed to watch her performance
and tell her why she hasn't been chosen in all the times she's
tried out for these kinds of shows."

"She should be the one watching you," he said quietly.

Something in his tone, in the way he almost whispered to
her, made Lori's skin tingle. "I don't understand," she said,
looking up at him. "Why?"

"Because you're going to be chosen," Jason said. "I'd be
willing to bet on it."

Lori sneaked a peek at her watch. Noon! No wonder she
was starving. They'd all been moved into a larger room and
put to work answering a list of questions, but she'd had no
idea so much time had passed. It was hardly surprising that
her stomach was growling like an angry bear emerging from
hibernation!

Looking surreptitiously at Annette, seated to her left,
Lori wasn't surprised to see that her friend was oblivious to
anything but the written test before her and was paying no
attention to Lori's embarrassing rumblings. She quickly
glanced around the room. Thank goodness. Apparently no
one else had noticed, either.

Maybe there was some forgotten tidbit lurking in the
depths of her purse, Lori thought. Rummaging among the
tattered coupons and loose coins, her fingers felt the

smooth, sticky remnants of one cherry candy, but when she saw it was covered with lint, she couldn't bring herself to eat it, no matter how hungry she was.

A long shadow fell over the clipboard in Lori's lap and she looked up to see Jason standing directly in front of her. He was holding what had been a roll of breath mints. There was one left.

Lori felt a warm blush begin to color her cheeks as she accepted his offering, discarding the wrapper into the already disastrous clutter of her handbag, and popping the tiny mint into her mouth. "I was trying to be subtle," she said quietly. "But thanks. My stomach is positive I've forgotten it."

"We should break for lunch soon," he said. "How are you coming on the questionnaire?"

"No problem," Lori told him. "I finished it about ten minutes ago."

"Me, too. I found it rather interesting, didn't you?"

Lori noticed she was getting disgusted glances from the overly quiet young man seated to one side of her, so she stood to speak more privately to Jason.

Hugging the clipboard to her chest, she smiled up at him. "Some of it was pretty personal. I had expected to play word games or anagrams or something like that, not to be asked to relate the story of half my childhood and most of my recent life."

Smiling, Jason held out his hand for her clipboard. "May I?"

"Well, I don't know if I should."

He shrugged. "Never mind. I can learn all I want to know about you by asking."

Lori felt her stomach tie in what had to be a triple-looped bow. And this time the knots were not from hunger. Her pulse had sped up and her knees were growing suspiciously weak in spite of her excellent physical condition. She was being ridiculous, she lectured herself. In a little while she would drive home, begin her vacation, and the Hollywood world Annette coveted so deeply would be in the past. Forgotten. So what difference could it possibly make if an attractive man was openly curious about her? she asked herself. And what harm could there be, as long as she didn't take him seriously?

"I won't guarantee I'll answer." Feigning a serene composure, Lori clutched the clipboard tighter.

Jason tried his best to look nonchalant and to put her at ease. "I'm really a nice guy when you get to know me."

"Except there's no chance of that," Lori said.

He glanced down at her left hand. "Are you one of those modern married women who refuses to wear a ring?"

"No. I'm single."

"Then what's the problem?"

"I just don't let men pick me up. Especially men I don't know." Lori knew she was beginning to sound pompous, but she wanted him to understand that it was no reflection on him. As a matter of fact, she wished they had met under different circumstances; somewhere where they could have gotten to know each other comfortably.

She had expected him to be offended. Instead, he began to grin. "You're a very wise lady, Lori. It's been an honor to meet you." *I knew you were that kind of woman,* he added silently.

"And you have no idea how good that makes me feel," she said. "Even the people I come in contact with through my work usually don't understand."

"I'll bet you're good at whatever it is you do," Jason responded. "I can't see you being less than perfect at any job."

He's the one who's good, Lori thought. Very good. She hadn't heard anyone quite so convincingly glib in a long time. Such talent deserved its reward. "Okay. Your smooth compliments have done me in. I teach aerobics and yoga."

"No wonder you look so trim and fit." Jason let his gaze travel slowly over her five-foot-six-inch frame while he savored each curve.

Flustered by his unashamed, assessing stare, Lori sought to redirect his thoughts. "And I'll bet, judging from your quick recovery at the elevator, that you either work out or have a favorite sport you practice regularly. Am I right?"

"Yes. Thanks."

"No thanks necessary. I appreciate someone who keeps himself in shape. It's part of my job to judge a person's physical fitness and offer advice."

Lori was trying to keep her active imagination in check and to censor her thoughts about him as if he were only a client, but she wasn't having a lot of success. He was someone she would like to know better—much better—and there was no getting around that fact. As soon as he spoke again, she realized she hadn't completely quelled her whimsical daydreaming.

"Maybe you could evaluate my performance sometime."

Lori's heart began to race, making her light-headed and speechless, a predictable reaction to the vividly sensual picture Jason had conjured up. She knew he hadn't meant anything personal when he'd mentioned "performance," but all she could think of now was Jason Daniels's strong, lithe body and the wonderful muscle control she could tell he possessed. Worse yet, all her platitudes about not letting a man pick her up were about to be negated by the bright red blush stealing up her cheeks!

The first indication Jason had that his statement had been misinterpreted was the rosy color flooding Lori's face. His words flashed through his mind and their intended meaning gave way to a more earthy analysis.

She found her voice. "I beg your pardon?"

Jason thought the whole exchange humorous, but he decided to continue a facade of innocence. He nodded, stony faced. "I've been having a lot of trouble with my serve lately."

"Your what?" She blinked and stared at him, but her thoughts refused to focus. Her usually quick wit was caught in a morass of turbulent feelings intertwined with shockingly explicit thoughts about Jason's body. Her brain had turned to soggy cardboard.

"You know. Tennis."

"I'm afraid I don't play," was all she could think to reply.

Jason watched the emotional volleyball of her thoughts, easily convincing himself that he deserved to enjoy a genuine good time with lovely Lori Kendall. Lord knows he'd have little enough chance to loosen up and be himself in the days to come.

Feigning seriousness, he took her hand. "It never crossed my mind that you would. I knew **you** were a nice girl from the moment I made you stop trying to pick up men by the elevator."

Lori couldn't believe he was teasing. Yet he had to be. Perhaps he had been from the first. She stared up at him, felt him gently squeeze her fingers and saw the corners of his firm mouth begin to twitch. In seconds, he was laughing softly and she had joined him.

"I don't know who you are or where you come from," Lori said, "but I'd hate to have to decide whether or not you were telling the truth." She shook her head incredulously. "Are you a lawyer?"

"More like a con man," he said candidly.

Lori opened her mouth to question him further, but loud applause from the other contestants at Simone's return kept her quiet.

Silently Jason turned and strode back across the room to his chair.

Brushing her skirt into place under her, Lori sat down. No matter what he really did for a living, Jason Daniels was certainly the most attractive, appealing man she'd met in a long time.

Yet something about him puzzled her. It was as if he were two separate people; pleasantly amusing when he was concentrating on her, but lapsing quickly into seriousness as soon as they parted.

Lori took a deep breath and released it with a sigh as she folded her hands in her lap. She knew she was being silly, but she wanted to cross the room to be near Jason again, to enjoy his captivating smile and see the mischievous gleam in his eyes when he teased her.

If every chair in the room hadn't been occupied, she'd have done just that.

Chapter Two

At the door Simone raised her hand. "If you'll all line up, you can pass your clipboards to me on your way to lunch. We have a catered buffet waiting in the office next door."

Lori's exclamation of relief was echoed by nearby contestants.

Annette jumped up and cut ahead of Lori in the line that was forming. "Did you answer all those questions? There were some that didn't make any sense to me at all."

Lori glanced over her shoulder to see where Jason was, hoping he was close by and disappointed when she realized he wasn't. "The questions I had didn't seem so tough. Maybe I misunderstood what I was supposed to do."

"Yeah." Annette batted at her hair to make it stand even farther away from her head. "It was hard to decide whether they wanted you to be clever, or what. I mean, like those stories about a certain situation where they asked you how you'd react. How do they expect us to know?"

"I just answered in the way that seemed right," Lori said. "Like the one about the old man and what you'd do if you were his landlord and found out he had a dog in his apartment against house rules."

"That one was easy," Annette said. "I'd change the rules so he could keep it there."

Lori wondered if there was a right or wrong answer. She hurried to keep up with Annette as they entered the room where lunch had been spread out. Not that her answers to the questions mattered, Lori thought. It was just nice to know when you were right. Providing you were, of course.

Two rows of tables with colored plastic cloths bisected the room. There were no place cards, so securing a seat became a sort of civilized free-for-all. Annette dropped her purse into a chair, reached for Lori's purse and plunked it into the chair beside hers. A line had already formed for the buffet and the two women joined it at the end.

Then Lori felt the hairs on the back of her neck prickle and she knew without looking who had stepped up behind her. The room was beginning to seem awfully warm and her bones were liquefying like candle wax beneath a flame.

There was no way she could have ignored Jason, even if she'd wanted to. And she certainly *didn't* want to. She turned and looked up at him. "Hi."

"Hi, again."

"I guess we're fated to spend a little more time together, huh?"

"I had already decided that." He smiled slightly. "Some things are inevitable."

"You don't have to make it sound quite so much like you're suffering," Lori complained pleasantly. "I'm not as bad as you seem to think."

"On the contrary," Jason said. "I find you extraordinary. It's just that people in situations like this are prone to lose touch with reality and I'm trying not to follow suit. I guess the glitter and glamour of the Hollywood scene affect all of us more than we suspect."

"From con man to philosopher." As they reached the food table, Lori picked up plates and silverware for them both, handing him one set. "I would like to know who and what you are, though, before we leave here so I can quit guessing."

Jason accepted her offering, gently guiding her ahead of him and balancing his empty plate with the other hand. "If I thought it would do me any good, I'd gladly tell you," he said. "However, in my case, I can see no point in carrying our friendship any further."

"You mean, because we'll never see each other again?"

"Yes," Jason lied.

Ah, just as she suspected, he was in California on vacation. Lori looked up at him, her eyes searching his face for the sign she knew must be there, however deeply buried. No matter how unlikely their relationship might be, no words would convince her Jason wasn't feeling the same sensations she was.

"I don't suppose you're going to be staying long in California?" she asked.

"Beg pardon?"

"You. Here. I've gathered you're a visitor and I assumed you were here on vacation. Am I right?"

He hesitated only a split second before deciding to skip an awkward explanation of his recent move and career changes. "Yes. I'm from Chicago."

"Where you're a well-known ax murderer, right?"

"Something like that." Jason helped himself to lettuce, then heaped alfalfa sprouts, avocado slices and garbanzo beans on top of it before drenching the whole pile in Italian dressing.

Watching him, Lori laughed. "You may be from Illinois, but you definitely eat like a native Californian." She stepped forward in line. "Here. Have some quiche, too. It'll complete the image and totally destroy my preconceived ideas about you."

"Which were?" Jason asked, steadying his plate so she could serve him.

Lori decided her safest answer was a patent fib. "A meat-and-potatoes kind of guy who lives in an old brick house on a quiet, shady street, runs the local hardware store, drives a Buick sedan—green—and goes to church every Sunday, except when the football games are on TV in the fall. A steady character."

Her *real* impression was far different. She could easily picture Jason as a buccaneer with a patch over one eye, swinging from the yardarm and brandishing a sword, while maidens swooned at his feet and brave men quailed in his presence.

"Is that what you like in a man, Lori?"

She laughed lightly. "If I knew what I liked, I don't suppose I'd still be single at twenty-eight."

"Maybe you've just been unlucky."

"Or lucky." Lori shrugged her shoulders. "My mother says I'm too particular. Seems to me, I'm rather clever to have avoided the mistakes so many of my friends have made." Finishing the buffet line by choosing a piece of cheesecake, she paused while Jason did the same, then led him to the seats Annette had reserved.

Jason added a chair to the table next to Lori, politely apologizing to the young man who had to scoot over to make room. He noticed Annette's elbow in her friend's ribs and her smile of obvious delight, but his concentration was focused on Lori. "I don't think you're too particular," he said. "I think you're very wise. I just wish..."

Lori leaned forward as his last words trailed off. "Yes?"

"Nothing," Jason said, laying his napkin across his lap. "I was daydreaming. It's nothing."

He looked so serious yet vulnerable, it was hard for Lori to keep from touching his hand to comfort him. Only the thinly veiled warning in his eyes and his tense posture kept her from actually doing it.

* * *

Dessert, Lori soon learned, was cheesecake *and* a speech. She listened politely while Simone reintroduced Vicki, an older woman with "capability" stamped unmistakably all over her; serious dark eyes, a no-nonsense hairstyle and ultracasual, obviously expensive clothing. Vicki reminded Lori of Mrs. Fensterwald, the English teacher who had single-handedly seen to it that the entire varsity football team passed her class with nothing less than a genuinely earned *B*!

"Now that you have all taken the written test," Vicki said, "we'll be going back into the other office to play some word and puzzle games."

Annette groaned audibly.

Vicki's instant scowl startled Lori. Looking around the room, she saw that almost everyone else had the same negative reaction. Annette was now cringing visibly.

"You're all here because you wanted to be, not because anyone forced you," Vicki reminded them. "Our initial contestant testing will take longer this time than it will once the show is produced and viewers have seen it played." She held her hands out, palms up. "I'm sure you can all understand that."

Jason brushed Lori's arm fleetingly. "*Almost* everyone is here because they wanted to be," he said.

Glancing at Vicki to be sure she hadn't heard his comment, Lori smiled at him. "I love a challenge. I wouldn't quit now under any circumstances. It sounds like fun."

On cue, Vicki reinforced Lori's ideas. "We'll be watching you, yes, but I also expect you to loosen up, be yourself and have a good time. That's the only way we can get an accurate picture of your performance. Now, shall we go?"

Annette had begun to fidget. As the contestants filed out of the room, she nudged Lori. "I almost blew it, didn't I? Geez-louise, I hope she doesn't hold a grudge."

"I suspect she'd choose a good player over any personal like or dislike she might have. Vicki strikes me as totally committed to her job." Lori looked up at Jason, who had joined them. "Don't you agree?"

"I do." He stuffed his hands into his pockets to keep himself from reaching for Lori. He'd unthinkingly touched her arm when he'd whispered to her and the ends of his fingers still tingled from the contact.

You're working, damn it, Jason told himself. Leave her alone. But his subconscious wasn't willing to let him break away. Perhaps the games Vicki had planned for later would take the burden of choice from him, he reasoned. Part of him actually hoped so.

Jason's jaw clenched. All things considered, this was going to be a hell of a long day.

Lori's next glimpse of the large room where they had begun their testing surprised her. While the group had been at lunch the seating had been rearranged. Now there were rows in the back, as in a theater, and four chairs in the front, facing the rest. Vicki stood by the four chairs with the now-familiar stack of yellow cards and photos, shuffling through them quickly and silently while everyone assembled in the room. With a wave of her arm, she indicated that they should be seated.

Lori led the way, found three empty chairs together and was chagrined when Annette plunked herself down next, instead of allowing Jason the seat in the middle. She peeked around Annette's fuzzy hairdo and caught him smiling to himself.

"All right. I'd like to see Chuck, Val, Lori and Steve," Vicki said. "Come up here and sit in one of these chairs."

Smiling anxiously, Lori laid aside her purse and glanced at Annette. Her friend was frowning, rather than sending her encouragement. Jason, on the other hand, was nodding, smiling at her and giving her a thumbs-up sign. How sweet, Lori thought. How gallant. As her stomach did back flips and her palms began to perspire, Lori took her place in one of the four chairs.

Using a stopwatch, Simone kept time while Vicki rapidly fired a series of words, first at Val, then at Steve. Some of the quickest answers were the funniest because no one could answer in time and still carefully consider what to say. Or, more importantly, what *not* to say.

Chuck, the third one to try, said, "Sex," in response to "Cookies," and everyone was still laughing when Lori's turn came.

She sat rigidly in the chair, her clammy hands folded on her lap, and listened intently to Vicki.

"Okay," Vicki said. "You understand what we're after and you can see how much fun it can be if you'll just say the first thing that comes into your head. Right?"

Lori nodded.

"Okay. Ready? Fifteen seconds." Vicki nodded to Simone to start the stopwatch. "Go."

Lori knew that Vicki had been speaking to Simone, but she herself was so nervous and caught up in the spirit of the game that she immediately responded with "Proceed," to everyone's delight.

"Clever," Vicki said while Simone laughed for the first time since they'd arrived.

"Smart," Lori cracked back.

Vicki was shaking her head and chuckling. "I've been doing this sort of thing for eight years and every once in a while someone comes along who takes even me by surprise. All right, Lori. Now, let's play the game the right way, shall we?"

"Yes, ma'am." Visions of Mrs. Fensterwald were dancing in Lori's head.

Stifling a smile, Vicki said, "Help."

The word *me* popped into Lori's mind, but she answered with "Teach," compliments of Fensterwald.

"Eyes."

Lori pictured Jason's darkly appealing gaze, yet she knew she didn't dare mention his name, not if she hoped to confine the color of her cheeks to a moderately demure blush. "Magic," she said, managing to respond in a split second and forestall a lecture about not taking time to think first.

"Sorcerer," Vicki went on, raising her eyebrows and watching Lori.

Oh, no! Ever since Lori had run into Jason in the hallway she'd been envisioning him in a mysterious way. Now, all the words seemed to lead her to his name, his image. Come to think of it, everything brought him to mind, she realized with a start.

"Micky Mouse," she answered, remembering his part in the cartoon. Anything to get her thoughts off Jason.

"Sexy," Vicki said.

"Thank you," Lori quipped.

"Baloney."

"Sandwich."

"I quit," Vicki said, smiling. She addressed the entire group. "As you can see, some of us give rather unusual responses. What we propose to do in the show is have teams of three members. One member will go through a similar list of words while on camera, then the others will be brought in to guess which responses belong to his or her partner. That will be round one. The second round will consist of rebus puzzles and in the third round each person will be given a set of clues and asked to follow them to a final prize location. Sort of like an old-fashioned scavenger hunt. Each round will be scored separately and the final tally will determine the winning team."

Vicki excused the first four players and began to call up others while Annette fidgeted. When her name was finally called, Jason used the opportunity to change seats and move next to Lori.

"You did quite well," he told her.

She couldn't keep from blushing, considering what she had almost said regarding him. "Thanks. I was awfully nervous."

"You hid it beautifully. I think even Vicki was surprised."

"You really think so? It *was* fun." She looked at Annette, watching her struggle with her answers under Vicki's strong delivery. "I guess there's something to be said for not being too desperate to get on the show."

"I suppose." He paused, leaning closer. "You mean you wouldn't accept if you were chosen?"

"Of course not."

"That hardly seems fair to Vicki and her staff, does it? They've invested time and money in testing you."

"I see your point."

"And then there's the business of Vicki's job and reputation. I'm sure she has a lot riding on her ability to find suitable contestants."

"I guess I didn't see it quite that way before," Lori said. "The problem is, if I was picked and Annette wasn't, it might hurt our friendship."

"And if she made it, too?"

Lori stared up at Jason. He seemed to be borrowing trouble, creating impossible scenarios for no reason. No one could possibly know this early who would be chosen. And he seemed awfully concerned about Vicki's success, too. Oh, well, Lori thought, maybe he was the type of person who liked to solve life's puzzles so much that he invented them when none occurred naturally.

"I can't say what I'd do," Lori told him. "I usually wait for catastrophes to actually happen before I begin dealing with them."

The corners of his mouth quirked, and his dimple appeared. "Maybe that's why you're not married."

Lori smiled back at him. "You know, you just may be right." She stopped talking as Annette rejoined them.

"Did you hear what I said?" Annette asked with a groan. "I was awful. I know I was." Pausing in front of Lori, she cocked her head to one side and furrowed her brow. "I think you're sitting in my seat."

"No. Jason is," Lori told her.

"Oh." Annette fell into the empty chair beside him as if she'd been shot, all the verve gone out of her. "I'm dead meat. I'll never get to play now. All this was for nothing."

Jason smiled amiably. "You can't be sure of that. According to Vicki, we still have the rebus and puzzle solving to try."

Annette looked up at him, cupped her hand around the side of her mouth and whispered, "I know. I think I caught a glimpse of some of the answers when Vicki laid my card down on the table." She batted her false eyelashes. "When all this is over, how about joining me for a drink?"

"You?" Frowning, Jason pulled away from her. "I thought you and Lori came together."

"Right. I mean, us. Will you join us?" Annette shot a meaningful glance toward Lori. "Of course, Lori doesn't drink, so I guess she wouldn't be interested. Besides, it's her vacation and she wants to go to the beach or something."

"Ah, the famous California beaches. I'd wanted to see those while I was out here on the West Coast." It was possible he could spend some private time with Lori and still preserve his true identity, he told himself. She already thought he was a tourist. If he tried to correct her mistaken conclusions at this late date, he'd only create more problems than he solved by making her doubt his overall veracity. Of course, he could wait, get Lori's home address from Vicki after the tryouts were over, and then telephone her. His conscious mind told him he should be sensible and wait. The trouble was, he didn't *feel* sensible. Not sensible at all.

Jason turned and focused his attention on Lori. "Would you mind showing a stranger a few of the sights?" He chuckled softly. "That is, if we get out of here while we're still young enough to enjoy them."

"I guess I could act as tour guide for a day or so." Lori's heart was threatening to beat its way out of her chest and she was thankful she was sitting because she knew her legs wouldn't support her in a standing position. After all his talk about never seeing her again, here he was, inviting her to spend time with him!

Ignoring the daggers in the look she was receiving from Annette, Lori fought to keep her smile from spreading so wide that she'd resemble the fabled Cheshire cat. So, Jason Daniels had changed his mind about her, had he? Well, she wasn't going to worry about why, or waste what promised to be a lovely time, thinking about whether she would ever see him again once he went back to Chicago. What counted was the here and now.

A wave of joy washed over Lori. Her current competition in the quiz-show tryouts paled compared to her anticipation of time spent in the company of Jason Daniels, and she wondered if he was looking forward to it with as much fervor.

The electrifying look in his eyes told her he was.

As the tiring afternoon wore on, Lori completed more written questions, this batch pertaining to the rebus part of the contest. She stretched her arms over her head to relieve her taut shoulder muscles, then lowered her hands to her lap with a sigh.

"Psst. Move your right hand. I can't see."

Frowning, Lori glanced at Annette. "What?"

"I said, move your hands."

"That's cheating."

"So? We're friends, aren't we?"

Lori sensed eyes on her, looked up and found Vicki watching. "Knock it off before we're both disqualified," Lori warned.

Annette pulled a face.

By smiling and leaving her hands folded demurely on the top of her test, Lori managed to keep Vicki from getting suspicious. As soon as the group was dismissed, Lori took Annette aside. "You almost blew it that time."

"Me?" Annette asked angrily. "You were the one who wouldn't help me."

"Besides the fact that it wasn't fair, we were being watched."

"So? You still could have moved so I could see. I spent the last ten minutes on question number twenty and never did figure out the answer."

Lori patted her friend on the back. "That's okay. Nobody said you had to be perfect to be chosen to play the real game." She joined the rest of the contestants filing out of the offices into the hall.

"Who's not perfect?" Jason asked, coming up behind them.

Lori yawned. "Well, I'm certainly not. If this session had gone on much longer, I know I'd have dozed off for sure."

"Sleeping Beauty," he said.

Annette stepped to the opposite side of him. "Know where we can find a handsome prince?"

"Annette Cole!" Lori felt a heated rush of color flood her cheeks.

Chuckling, Jason graciously offered each woman an arm. Annette grasped the one extended to her immediately.

Then he turned to Lori, smiled and took her hand instead, and she accepted his friendly gesture without hesitation.

"I had no idea so much stamina was required for such a simple game," she said. "And Simone says we still have to wait for Vicki's phone call to find out who was chosen and who wasn't. I can't believe it!"

"I'm not tired at all," Annette said. "Let's hit some of the clubs on Sunset Boulevard."

Jason squeezed Lori's hand as he shook his head. "Sorry. I'm much too worn out for a night on the town. Jet lag, I think." He stepped back to let them board the elevator ahead of him. "I'll walk you two to your car and see you safely off. Then, I'm for going to bed early."

Lori blushed as Annette giggled, "But, Jason, I hardly know you." Laughing to herself, Annette directed a rambling monologue about game shows, contestant searches and life in general, at the captive audience of strangers in the elevator.

Jason shook his head and smiled at Lori. "Your friend is so overtired she's getting silly. I suspect she'll be asleep before either of us, as soon as her extra jolt of adrenaline wears off. She was awfully tense during the tryouts."

"I agree."

Lowering his voice, he added, "How shall I get in touch with you?"

"You were serious, then."

"Of course. I can't imagine getting a California sunburn without you."

Lori looked at his dark coloring and smiled. "Something tells me you're the lucky kind who doesn't burn."

"Actually I spend as much time out-of-doors as I can, even in the winter," Jason said. "Long hours in an office are worse for you if there's no relief from the tensions and the stale air."

She began to grin at him. "That's better. So, go ahead. Tell me about yourself and what kind of an office you work in."

"It's not that interesting, Lori. Besides, I'm on vacation, remember? I don't want to talk shop when I'm here to relax." He led the way to the outer door on the ground floor and held it open.

Lori bestowed a pleasant smile on the uniformed guard who bid them good-night, thanking him for his good-luck wishes. The summer sun was still a long way from setting and the sidewalk was bathed in a glow from the rays that peeked between the tallest buildings and warmed her comfortingly.

"Ummm." She breathed deeply. "It feels good out here. The air-conditioning in that building made it kind of chilly."

Looking around them, Jason raised one eyebrow. "I'd heard there were all kinds of strange souls wandering the streets here in Hollywood. Where are they?"

"It's a little too early for the craziest people," Lori volunteered. "But if you change your mind and decide to stick with Annette, she'll see to it you hit all the high spots."

"And if I stick with you?"

Lori blushed. "My car is parked on the next block in the Cinerama Dome lot." She pointed. "Behind the theater." Reaching into her purse, she produced a pink-and-white business card and handed it to Jason as they walked. "Here's my number. I can usually be reached in the evenings."

She chewed on her lower lip. Why, oh why, had she put it *that* way? Now Jason would think she never went out, never had dates. That wasn't true. Not exactly. Her social life was limited, but that was by her own choice. She rejected the suggestion that she was looking for the perfect man, yet had to admit there was a shade of truth in the idea. After all, her ultimate choice would last forever. Such a decision couldn't be taken lightly.

Glancing at Jason as he studied the card, Lori felt her pulse gaining speed. If she hadn't been so in tune with the workings of her body, she might have suspected she was experiencing palpitations or some other physical problem. But she knew better. Her heart was in fine shape, as was the rest of her body. No, there was nothing wrong with her that getting away from Jason Daniels wouldn't cure. Of course, getting closer to him would also provide a cure one way or another, her mind argued logically. Was that what she wanted? Darned if she knew. Getting to know him wasn't sensible. Appealing, yes, but probably not very smart.

Annette yawned loudly and led the way past the lethargic parking-lot attendant to Lori's Mustang. Bringing up the rear, Lori and Jason walked slowly, letting Annette draw farther and farther ahead.

"Look," Lori said quietly, not wanting him to feel compelled to see her again. "If you change your mind, I won't be angry. I mean, I know how it is with men. Sometimes they mean well, but never get around to phoning. I don't want you to think you're in any way obligated."

"Don't you?" Jason paused. "I was hoping you'd be desolate if I didn't keep in touch."

"How about mildly disappointed?" Lori asked, smiling up at him and realizing she would be disappointed if he didn't call.

"I'll settle for that." She was so pretty, so desirable, standing there looking at him with those big, trusting eyes of hers, Jason couldn't bring himself to part from her. Not without demonstrating how attractive he thought she was.

He spoke more softly. "I don't suppose you'd like me to kiss you goodbye?"

She knew her lips had parted slightly and softened at his suggestion. And she was positive he had noticed the change in her because his own mouth looked somehow more tender, more ready.

Jason released her hand and let his fingers trail a tingling path up her arm. Standing there with the summer sunlight reflecting in her chestnut-colored hair, Lori Kendall was the most beautiful woman he had ever seen. His other hand came to rest gently on her shoulder.

"That's an unfair question," she said.

"But a necessary one."

"Is it?" Lori smiled slightly. Placing her hands lightly on his chest, she raised herself onto her toes.

Jason's lips descended in slow motion, the feather-light brushing of his mouth on hers no more than a sweet promise of things to come.

Overcome by the enchantment of his kiss, Lori knew she was behaving contrary to her own strict rules of conduct, yet she refused to listen to the rational arguments coming from the sensible side of her brain. At that moment, if Jason Daniels had picked her up in his arms and carried her off, she knew she would have done nothing to dissuade him.

In seconds, the magic of his touch was withdrawn. Jason faced her, his eyes searching hers with unspoken questions. Then he grasped her shoulders firmly, pushing her away.

"I think I just made a big mistake," he said, his voice low and husky. "Hell, I *know* I did."

Lori stared silently into the fathomless depths of his dark gaze. Whatever magic he possessed, it was clear he certainly knew how to apply it to his kisses. She had no idea what he'd meant about making a mistake, nor did she care. That one kiss had been no mistake on *her* part, of that she was certain, and the only regret she had was that he had ended it so quickly.

Asserting her own self-control, Lori took a deep breath and retreated. Slowly, tentatively, her hands fell to her sides. The last of her reservations about letting herself become involved with someone from so far away had disappeared in the cloud of emotion and body chemistry contained in Jason's kiss.

Lori fantasized for an instant that Jason really was going to sweep her up in his arms and carry her off. Instead, he took her firmly by the arm and escorted her to the car where Annette waited, mouth agape, eyes wide.

"I'll call you," he said. Taking the key from Lori's shaking hand he fitted it into the door lock, opened the door and helped her in, then went around the car to do the same for Annette. Returning to Lori, he handed her the keys through the now-open window, turned wordlessly and walked away.

Watching him go, Lori tried to recapture the feeling of his lips on hers, the warmth of his body as they had stood close together. Instead, she felt a knot of longing in her core. A few seconds ago, she had visualized Jason capturing her like a vanquished princess. Now, in spite of his promise to call, he was acting as if he were departing for good, and Lori's sense of loss amazed her.

Annette grabbed her arm, waking her from her daydream. "Geez-louise, what was that all about? My God, he kissed you, Lori! How did that happen?"

"It beats me," Lori said with a wistful smile. "But I'm sure glad it did."

"I couldn't believe my eyes! One minute he's talking to us and the next minute you and he are lip-to-lip in broad daylight! And you said *I* was too extroverted."

"I may have been wrong," Lori said, still pensive. "It looks like I may have been wrong about a lot of things."

"Like what?"

"Like men," Lori said. "I thought I understood them perfectly. Now, I'm not so sure."

Chapter Three

Jason returned to the closed office building he had just left, knocked on the glass doors for the guard's attention, showed his studio ID and was admitted. The empty elevator took him quickly back to the seventh floor, where he met Vicki and Simone.

"Sorry I'm late. I thought it better to avoid suspicion by leaving with the rest of the contestants."

Vicki eyed him dubiously. She led the way to an inner office where fifteen yellow cards were spread out on a desk. Jason's was among them.

"I probably wouldn't pick you out of this batch if I didn't have to," Vicki said. "You're too serious. And too good-looking."

He ran one hand over his hair and sighed. "Meaning?"

"The girls in the contestant pool have already noticed you. That kind of behavior can ruin a good game."

"I'll take care of that," Jason said. "Besides, I don't expect to be involved in this operation during the whole show. McAlister wants me to sit in and report. That's all. Shouldn't take long."

He stooped over the desk, scanning the cards, removed one and handed it to Simone. "Let's leave this person out, shall we?"

Vicki snatched it away. "Lori Kendall? Oh, no! She's one of my best players." Scowling, the older woman stared at Jason. "I thought I sensed something going on between you two." She started to smile. "Well, your hormones are your problem, not mine."

"You're all heart," Jason said.

"No, I'm all business, and I suggest you remember that if you expect to survive as long as I have."

Jason gritted his teeth. Vicki was right, but that didn't make the situation any easier to take. Frustrated, he thrust his hands into his pockets. The worst part was, *he* was the fool who had talked Lori into fulfilling her obligations if she was chosen to play!

Terrific, Daniels, he grumbled to himself. Nice work. If Vicki was as predictable as he thought she was, he and Lori would wind up playing on the same team when the taping began.

"When can I expect to hear from you?" he asked.

"Simone will be making the notifications in a few days. In the meantime, we'll have a psychologist go over the answers to the hypothetical questions." Vicki smiled to herself. "I don't expect any surprises, though. I'm usually right when it comes to choosing contestants."

"I'd like to see the results, if you don't mind."

She smiled knowingly. "Of course. I'll have copies delivered to Affiliated Broadcasting. What name?"

"Send them to Brad Fox in Fair Practices. He'll get them to me."

"As you wish. We at Halpern-Oldham are always glad to help the networks."

Jason turned on his heel and stalked out. He couldn't blame Vicki for being sarcastic. Everyone in the business knew there was no love lost between those whose job it was to put on the shows and those entrusted with policing the activity. Still, it was going to be damn inconvenient for him. He laughed to himself. Inconvenient was hardly the right word for what he was feeling. All his life he'd searched for someone just like Lori Kendall and now...

Damn it all. How could he do his job and still get to know Lori? Or more precisely, how could he follow his natural urges without jeopardizing his career?

Cursing under his breath, Jason rode the elevator to the street level, took Lori's business card out of his pocket, found the nearest telephone booth, and listened impatiently to the rings on the other end of the line.

"Idiot," Jason told himself. "She couldn't be home yet. She just left here ten minutes ago." Hanging up the receiver, he checked his watch. He'd give her another hour, then try again.

Jason made a wry face as he sipped from the half-empty cup of lukewarm coffee he'd been nursing in the small restaurant. Well, he grumbled to himself, at least he'd managed to kill twenty minutes. Fidgeting, he spotted a pay telephone by the door, left a generous tip for the harried waitress and yielded to the compulsion to try Lori's number once again.

He was about to give up after fifteen rings when she answered, obviously out of breath. "Hello?"

For a few long seconds, Jason found himself speechless. "I—uh, I'm sorry," he finally said. "You don't sound like yourself."

Smiling, Lori dropped her purse onto the table, kicked off her shoes and sank into a chair. "I just this minute walked in and heard the phone ringing. Traffic on the freeway was horrendous."

"Sorry if I bothered you. I wanted to talk to you again."

"Well, you certainly do keep your promises," Lori said. "I was afraid—"

"I know. I shouldn't have left you so abruptly."

"That's okay," she told him. "I'm sure you had your reasons."

Jason cleared his throat. "I think we should talk about my reasons, Lori, because I have an idea that our little kiss affected you the same way it did me. Am I right?"

Glad she was already sitting down, Lori leaned against the chair for support. "I liked it, if that's what you mean." She giggled nervously. "You should have seen the look on Annette's face when you walked away. It was priceless."

"There are things I'd very much like to share with you about myself, Lori. The trouble is, I'm not at liberty to do so."

"The last man who talked to me that way was married," Lori said. "Are you?"

"No."

"And you aren't really an ax murderer, either?"

"No." He was beginning to chuckle. "I'm one of the good guys. Honest, I am."

"Then I fail to see the problem."

"What if we spend time together and become, shall we say, 'close'? It might be very difficult for you, not knowing much about me."

She was smiling into the empty room, thinking about growing closer to Jason Daniels. The idea definitely appealed to her. "You're single, law-abiding and healthy?"

"Yes," Jason said. "I'm so pure you'd think I had a permanent halo stationed above my ears."

"That would be cute." Lori chose her next words carefully. "It seems to me that you're borrowing trouble, Jason. Who knows? We might spend a few hours together and find out we don't get along at all." The sound of his warm laugh thrilled her.

"Is that what you really think?"

"Hardly." She sighed. "How long will you be staying in California before you have to be back in Chicago?"

Jason took a distracted breath. The more he said to her the bigger the lie grew. Soon, there would be no way to put their relationship on a firm foundation. Yet he had to act now. He didn't dare wait. He knew that once Vicki called Lori and the videotaping began, they'd be thrown together anyway. He was positive that his only alternative outside of walking away from Lori Kendall forever was to try to establish a friendship first and pray it would be strong enough to endure once the charade was over and Lori found out who and what he really was.

"I can squeeze out a few more weeks," Jason said. "How long is your vacation?"

"Counting today, I have fourteen days. That should be enough time to show you the evils of our beaches, for a start."

"I put myself in your hands, Ms. Kendall. Choose whatever you think will be fun and I'll go along."

Lori sighed deeply. She couldn't forget that Jason was a tourist, soon to depart for home. Surely no harm would be done by confiding her true feelings to him, since whatever developed between them in the weeks to come was doomed from the start by sheer distance.

"I think that just about anything we do together will be fun," she said.

Jason's voice was husky. "So do I, Lori. And I don't want to wait a minute longer than I have to. How about dinner?"

"Tonight? Now? I thought you had jet lag."

"It's only seven. I'll live. Honest I will."

How could she protest when she yearned so to be with him? It took only a moment to decide not to waste what little time they had. "My home address is on the card," Lori said. "I live in Monrovia, just north of the 210 freeway. Tell me where you're staying and I'll give you driving directions.''

Staying? Oh, damn, Jason thought. This stupid situation was getting more complicated by the minute. He'd stupidly let her go thinking he was a tourist and now he couldn't very well admit he had recently moved into a condominium in Santa Monica and drove a red Ferrari with California plates, compliments of Affiliated Broadcasting.

"I'll find it," Jason said. "Just be ready in an hour."

"You're sure about all this?"

"As sure as I've ever been," he said. "See you soon."

The receiver clicked into place as Jason reached for the yellow pages. Thumbing through the telephone directory, he found the number he needed.

A woman's voice bid him a pleasant, "Hello," followed by, "California Rentals. How may I help you?"

"My name is Daniels," he said. "I need to rent a specific kind of car and I need it immediately. Cost is no object."

"Yes, sir. If we don't have it in stock, I'll be glad to refer you to another establishment. What make and model do you require?"

"A Buick sedan," Jason said. "And it has to be green."

Lori paced the floor in her bare feet. She'd had second thoughts about welcoming Jason into her home as soon as he'd hung up the phone, but it was too late to do anything about it. She had no way to reach him or stop him from coming.

Not that she wasn't glad he'd called, she told herself. It was just that she'd been counting on her vacation time to do some heavy housecleaning and maybe even paint the exterior of her quaint old house. Consequently, she'd put off the daily straightening up that was a regular part of her routine.

Glancing around her cluttered living room with its braided rug, antique sofa and eclectic assortment of knickknacks, she thought seriously about locking the front door behind her and meeting Jason on the sidewalk by the curb to save face.

Lori laughed to herself. What real difference did it make whether or not he noticed the mess? If she couldn't relax and be herself in the company of a man she'd never see again, then when could she? Besides, she knew her home didn't always look like news footage of a tornado's aftermath. And it was her vacation.

Unfortunately she hadn't thought to ask Jason what type of restaurant he wanted to patronize. Well, she was bone tired, the house was a disaster area, her wardrobe was made up mainly of casual, California-style clothing and she knew she couldn't do everything to perfection by the time he arrived, so she opted for the easy way out.

She showered quickly, then chose a sundress in a bold Hawaiian print with bright pink, lavender and coral flowers resting on a deep blue background. She ran a brush through her hair, then began to hurry around the house, putting away the most embarrassing of the personal items that were strewn everywhere.

A muffled whine and scratching at the back door reminded her she had overlooked her pal, Muggsy. The little dog had wandered into her yard a scant three months ago, hopped up onto her porch swing, curled into a secure, shaggy ball and made himself at home.

Lori smiled, remembering how she had advertised for his owner and put notices up on local supermarket bulletin boards, hoping with all her heart that no one would claim her newfound pet. Luckily, no one had.

She started for the back door to let Muggsy in when she heard a car stopping in front of the house. Under her left arm was the as-yet-unread daily newspaper; her other arm was crammed with laundry on its way to the washer in the service porch and it looked as if Jason was already here.

"Oh, rats," Lori muttered. She stashed the newspaper under the cushions of the overstuffed couch, tossed her laundry inside her bedroom doorway, closed the door and went to answer Jason's knock.

Impatient to be welcomed, Muggsy also made his way to the front of the house. The clever little fur ball hit the porch at a dead run, just as Lori opened the door, and darted through the opening so fast his tawny coat was nothing more than a blur.

Jason smiled. "Hello." He cocked his head. "What was that? A comet with hair?"

"No. That was Muggsy. He has the idea he lives inside. I keep trying to persuade him outside is better."

"He doesn't seem convinced."

"He isn't." Lori ushered Jason into her living room. "Can I get you something to drink? How about an iced tea?"

"Fine. No lemon." He glanced around the room. "This is nice. Just what I thought your place would be like."

The wreck of the Hesperus? Lori wondered. She smiled. "Is that a compliment?"

"Of course." Leaning down, Jason peered beneath the gateleg table.

"How about standing up straight and overlooking the dust devils?" Lori urged. "I was planning on doing my spring cleaning during my vacation."

"It's summer," Jason countered. "But I wasn't inspecting your housekeeping skills. I was looking for the little dog. Where did he go?"

Lori stared at her visitor with new admiration. "Most of my friends are glad when Muggsy disappears. Don't tell me you like him?"

"Sure. I like all animals. You said his name is Muggsy?"

"Uh-huh." She called to the little dog. "Hey, Muggsy, it's safe to come out. This one's friendly."

With a squeaky bark, Muggsy came sliding around the corner into the room and placed his furry body between Lori and Jason. Looking from one to the other, he danced in circles, panting gaily.

Jason scooped the dog up into his arms. "Hi, pal. What's the matter? You lonesome?"

Muggsy tried to lick Jason's face. Failing that, he settled for wagging his bushy tail and wriggling ecstatically at the special attention.

"I think he likes you," Lori said. "He's quite a clown and not too well-behaved, I'm afraid, but don't blame me. I've only had him for a few months. He showed up on my doorstep one day, tired and hungry, and he's been here ever since." Turning away, Lori started for the kitchen. "I'll go get your iced tea."

"Do you mind if I try to teach him a few things?" Jason called after her. "I used to have a mutt and I managed to train him pretty well."

Lori looked back at the grinning man and happy dog. They made quite a picture—almost as if they belonged together.

"I don't care. Just beware. He's *too* smart, sometimes." She saw Jason gently raise Muggsy's muzzle and look him in the eye. She added quickly, "And he loves to kiss people in the face."

Jason sputtered under the dog's assault. "Me, too, but I'd rather it was you, Lori."

She feigned misunderstanding. "Oh, Muggsy licks me all the time. Can't say I'm particularly fond of it, though." Laughing at Jason's perplexed expression, she left him alone with the dog.

When she returned with two tall glasses of iced tea, Lori was astounded to see Muggsy seated obediently at Jason's feet instead of crawling all over the furniture or racing around the room. "How did you—"

"Shush," Jason warned as she handed him one of the frosty glasses. "This is just the beginning and he could break concentration any second."

"He was fond of breaking my figurines whenever I went to work and left him in the house alone. That's why I have to make him stay out in the yard." She stared unbelievingly at Muggsy. The little dog wagged his tail for her, but kept his licorice-colored eyes trained on Jason.

"He needs a job to do," Jason said, slowly sipping his tea. "You know how frustrating it can be to be at loose ends all the time. Well, animals are like that, too. Our fuzzy friend here is more than happy to obey, once he knows the rules."

Lori shook her head. "Okay, Svengali. Explain. How could you get so far with him in such a short time?"

"I hate to take all the credit," Jason said. "I'm positive Muggsy has had some early training. All I did was revive his instincts and remind him of his manners."

"Which reminds me of mine," Lori said, sighing. "I'm so tired I wonder if you'd mind eating in a local restaurant instead of driving back into L.A.?"

Jason hadn't taken his eyes off Muggsy until now. As soon as he turned to set his half-empty glass on the table, the dog began prancing and spinning in circles. "What do you say we find an outdoor eatery and include our little friend?" Jason asked.

"You're kidding. Him? He'll wreck the place!"

"No, he won't. He'll be good. Won't you, boy?" Jason grinned. "I'll be responsible for him."

She couldn't help but smile at Jason's enthusiasm for taking the dog along. "And who will be responsible for you, Mr. Daniels?"

Jason scooped Muggsy up under one arm and put the other arm around Lori's waist, guiding her toward the door. "Gee, Ms. Kendall, I thought you were."

*   *   *

Carefully rolling up the car windows so there wasn't room for Muggsy to escape, Jason held the passenger door for Lori, got behind the wheel and released the little dog. Muggsy obligingly hopped over the front seat and made himself at home in the back as Jason started the car.

"He's a real trooper," Jason said. "I figured that anyone with a dog like him would take him for rides."

"In a green Buick?" Lori asked, smiling. "Can I ask you a personal question?"

"Sure."

"When did you rent this car? Was it before or after I mentioned my ideas about your life-style?"

Shrugging, Jason refused to be specific. "Let's just say I wanted to impress you properly and the car is part of my campaign."

"What makes you think I'm not the Ferrari or the Jaguar type?" She was watching his face as he drove and couldn't help noticing a warm blush rising beneath his collar. Afraid she had embarrassed him or made him feel uncomfortable she quickly added, "But you're right, of course. I'm not."

"Good." Jason glanced at the back seat, saw that Muggsy was all right and smiled at Lori. "I may be driving, but you're the native, remember? Where to?"

"There are several fast-food places and one garden restaurant that backs up to the street. If we eat there, Muggsy will have to stay in the car."

"And the other places? Can't we get our food and eat it in here with him?"

Lori looked at the plush interior of the rented car. "I guess so, if you're willing to pay to have the upholstery cleaned." She began to laugh softly, recalling her earlier worries about Jason seeing her untidy house.

He smiled at her. "What's so funny?"

"I am," Lori said. "You won't believe this, but I was scared to death to have you see my home for fear it might not be spotless enough for your tastes."

"My tastes? I don't quite understand."

"You know." She gestured toward his neatly pressed sport shirt and slacks. "You have the style of a junior executive, vacationing with the least formal garments in his wardrobe. I find myself expecting you to pull out a tie and suit coat any minute and become someone else."

Jason raised one eyebrow at her.

Smiling amiably, she patted his hand. "Don't worry. There's nothing wrong with looking neat and well put-together, especially if you're able to loosen up and have fun."

He faked a scowl. "You're telling me I'm stuffy, aren't you?"

"I'm saying I was wrong in thinking you might be a little too reserved," she said. "Any man who is willing to give up a fancy dinner to eat hamburgers with a fuzzy dog is okay in my book."

Grinning over at her, he chuckled. "I know. It works every time."

Now, it was Lori's turn to scowl. "What do you mean, every time?"

"Ladies," he said, looking very pleased with himself. "They get attached to their animals. All a man has to do to sneak into their hearts is make friends with the dog. It's so easy I should write a book about it."

She gave him a gentle poke that left him rubbing his arm. "Oh, yeah? Well, how many ladies have you tried your foolproof method on?"

"One." Jason was laughing quietly. "I'm sure it's going to become an important part of my repertoire, though."

"I'm sure it will," Lori said. "But for the present, let's concentrate on eating, shall we? I'm getting hungry."

The sun had come to rest on the hilly horizon and the summer breezes were cool as they blew through the partially open windows of the Buick. Reminded of childhood meals on the patio of the very house she now occupied, Lori made a snap decision.

"Look, Jason. I know you asked me out and I do expect a more formal dinner sometime, but how would you like to stop at a Chinese takeout and eat at home? It'll save the car from Muggsy and these summer evenings are perfect for meals served outdoors."

"I'd thought of something like that when I caught a glimpse of the table and chairs under those gorgeous trees by your house," Jason said, "but I was afraid you'd think I was stepping out of line for asking."

"So you put me in the position where I could hardly overlook the possibility? Whew! You're good, I'll say that for you."

"Am I still invited home?"

"Yes, you're still welcome." Lori was shaking her head and watching him closely. It wasn't that he appeared to be cocky or proud that he had gotten her to do what he'd wanted. On the contrary, Jason seemed to have finally relaxed. His hands didn't grip the wheel quite so tightly and his shoulders looked less tense than before. If Lori had been asked to name what she thought he was feeling, she would have to say it was immense relief, although why, she couldn't imagine.

Jason parked, gathered up the bulk of their dinner and headed for the house, followed by an adoring, obviously hungry dog.

Lori held open her front door, not bothering to fight Muggsy for the right to enter. "Bring the goodies out here, through the kitchen," she told Jason, "and I'll get a cloth for the patio table."

"Please, no fancy china, crystal or candles," he said in passing. "I didn't intend for you to work at this."

"Exactly what did you intend?" Lori asked. "I mean, here we are, alone in my home, and I barely know you. If I had any common sense, I'd be scared to death."

His voice was low and vibrant as he stepped up behind her. "I'd never hurt you, Lori. You must believe that."

She turned to face him and discovered he had set the bags of food on the counter. With nothing tangible to keep them apart, Lori could easily have fallen into his arms and she wondered vaguely why he wasn't making any move to embrace her. Boldly, she asked her question again. "What did you intend when you called me, Jason?"

"Not to take advantage of you, if that's what you mean."

Lori rested her hand on his arm and looked into his eyes. I could drown in the depths of those eyes, she thought, willing herself to search them for answers to the questions in her heart. What made Jason so determined to get to know her when there was no possible future in it? And why did he repeatedly grow serious in the midst of lighthearted conversations?

There was only one way to find out, she reasoned. Ask. But what was the use? She was positive she wouldn't get a straight answer from him.

Kindness and tenderness filled her. Whatever Jason's problem was, all she wanted was for him to be happy in her presence, in her home. Lori determined to raise his spirits and put his mind at ease.

"And I promise not to take advantage of you, either, Mr. Daniels. Even though I'm a physical-fitness expert, you have nothing to fear. As long as you behave yourself, I swear I won't throw you across the room or break any bones. At least not any important bones." She was pleased to see the seriousness fade from his face and a small smile take its place.

Muggsy had been jumping up and down at Lori's feet, begging for dinner. Now, he took hold of Jason's pants cuff, tugged hard on it and growled as if he'd just captured a dangerous burglar.

Jason reluctantly turned from Lori, reached down and picked up the little dog. "We temporarily forgot our dinner guest," he said. "All this came about because of Muggsy, and I'd swear he knows it."

Lori grinned at the twosome. "I think Muggsy's right. It's time we all ate."

With a nod, Jason leaned closer and brushed a light kiss against her cheek. "Keep reminding me how lucky I am to have met you, will you, honey? Sometimes I get too serious for my own good."

"Most of the time you're too serious for your own good," Lori agreed. "I don't suppose you'd like to tell me just what it is that's bugging you?"

"No."

"I thought not." She shooed him toward the bathroom. "Why don't you put Muggsy down and go wash for dinner?"

Watching him walk away, with the dog trotting faithfully at his heels, Lori was struck by the way Jason seemed to fit perfectly into her household, into her life. It was as if he had always been there, the perfect complement to everything in her home, to every facet of her daily living.

"You like intriguing things," she mumbled to herself, "like the armoire from Belgium and the one-of-a-kind, handmade mirror frame hanging on the entry wall."

Lori grew pensive. This was not a collection of unusual antiques she was thinking about. This was a man. And, boy, was that the truth, she added, blushing.

A now-familiar knot tied itself into loops in her lower abdomen and she closed her eyes against the certainty that Jason Daniels would soon vanish from her life.

Maybe his moods weren't so strange, after all, Lori mused. Maybe he had just been one step ahead of her in the realization that their special feelings would soon be lost in the vast distance between Chicago and southern California.

Lori wrapped her arms around her body and hugged herself. She could hear water running in the bathroom and the music of Jason's whistling above the background noise.

Suddenly she could hardly wait for him to rejoin her.

For a long time, Jason stood staring at his reflection in the bathroom mirror. So this is what a crazy man looks like, he mused. The woman in the next room was bound to cause him nothing but trouble, through no fault of her own, and he should jump in his rented car and drive away. Fast.

He smiled wryly at his image. There was no use kidding himself. He wasn't leaving. He hadn't felt this close to belonging somewhere, to someone, since he was a boy. A person didn't search for a lifetime for something, then abandon it just because there were complications. At least *he* didn't.

Jason dried his hands and hung the towel back on its rack. It wasn't often he'd walked into a strange place and felt suddenly at ease. Add to that the enticing presence of Lori Kendall, and he had the makings of a real home.

He wondered if she knew how deeply her genuine hospitality had affected him. Probably not.

Jason took a deep breath, made sure there was a smile on his face and prepared to rejoin her.

Chapter Four

Long evening shadows inched past Lori as she watched Jason lounging peacefully in the shade of the cottonwood trees surrounding her patio. A wisteria vine crept in gnarled splendor up the wall behind him. Clusters of pale purple flowers hung amongst its lush leaves like the decorations on a Christmas tree.

Lori leaned back. "The Mongolian beef and shrimp rice were delicious, but I'm stuffed." She looked at the clutter of empty paper plates and cardboard containers resting on her favorite coral tablecloth and sighed. "I should have stuck to my guns and insisted we use real china."

"Nonsense. All this is disposable. There's no need for you to go to extra work on my account. This is your vacation, remember?"

He reached for one of the fortune cookies and handed it to her. "Here. See what's in store for you."

Cracking the crisp cookie in half, Lori smiled at him. "I'm not much into fortunes or astrology. Don't you just hate it when somebody comes up to you and says, 'What sign are you?'"

"So, what do you tell them?"

"I usually try to point to one of those lighted exit signs they put over doors. It's good for a laugh." She glanced at the small, printed message in her hand. "Uh-oh."

"Bad news?"

Lori blushed. "You won't believe this. It says I'm going to meet a tall, handsome stranger and have twelve children."

"Let me see that fortune."

She jerked it away. "Oh, no. This one's private. You read yours."

Obligingly Jason straightened the slip of paper from his cookie. "You will meet a lovely lady and have twelve children."

"No way!" Lori lunged for his fortune, retrieved it and read, "You will soon go on a long journey." She looked at him from beneath her eyelashes. "I thought so."

Laughing with her, Jason leaned down and gave the last of their meal to Muggsy, smiling as the little dog gobbled it up.

Lori gazed at Jason across the table. "Do you still want to hit the beaches with me tomorrow? That can be your journey."

"Sure. We might as well make the most of both our vacations. That is, if you don't really mind."

"Not at all." Lori gave him an encouraging smile. "So, tell me, after you got your business degree where did you go?"

He shrugged. "No place interesting. I've worked in the investment field."

"And you have no brothers or sisters?"

"Like you, you mean? Heaven forbid! I don't know what I'd have done if I'd been the youngest of five children." He regarded her with awe. "It must have been hell."

"Not really." Lori was amused at his strong reaction to her confession that she was the baby in a large family. "My parents treated each of us as individuals. I think that made a lot of difference in our attitudes."

"Since you were the youngest, was there enough money to send you to college?"

"I spent some time in junior college, but I lost interest." Propping her bare feet up on an unused chair, Lori leaned back and closed her eyes. "You know, so many different things have fascinated me in my lifetime that I doubt any college could have kept up with my insatiable curiosity about the world around me."

She paused, then smiled at Jason. "Once I get to wondering about someone or something, I rarely quit until I learn the full story."

He knew his laugh sounded forced, but it was the best he could do. "Really? Maybe you've missed your calling. You should have been a detective."

Smiling demurely, Lori stood, stretched and began to clear the table. "I've often wished I could be really wise, like Sherlock Holmes. My grandmother was English, after all. I could sit and listen to her accent for hours, hanging on her every word."

Jason gathered up his plate and two of the empty cartons, then followed Lori into the house. "And she gave you this place?"

"Uh-huh." Setting the trash on the kitchen counter, Lori turned to face him. "Grandma knew how much I loved being here, so she left stocks and cash to each of my sisters, while I got the house."

"That pleased you?"

"Definitely." Lori leaned back against the porcelain-covered countertop. It was chipped and worn from years of hard usage, but she loved every nick, every crack. Her hand caressed the smooth edge. "You see this sink? It's an antique. I didn't have to buy it, and it's not only a conversation piece but also valuable to a collector. The whole house is like that."

She warmed to her subject, reaching out to grasp Jason's hand. "Come with me. I'll show you."

His grip was firm, and Lori felt happier in his presence than she ever had with anyone else.

She led him into the living room and paused by a tall oak highboy. "This piece was part of a set brought across the desert by my grandfather's grandmother. As the story goes, they had to abandon nearly everything they'd brought, but my great-great-grandmother refused to leave this behind. It had been a wedding present from her parents."

"And the hanging lamp?" Jason asked. "It looks valuable, too."

"It is. It's a genuine Tiffany. It was a gift from my grandfather to my grandmother on their twenty-fifth wedding anniversary."

"It's kind of amazing to look back on the past and see how marriages lasted in those days, isn't it?" Jason commented thoughtfully. "My parents split up when I was pretty young."

"That makes it tough to visualize a long-lasting relationship, doesn't it? I always swore I'd never marry anyone whose home life had been disrupted like that." She felt his grip tighten for a second before he abruptly released her hand.

"Why?"

"Because it's important. I'd certainly think twice before getting serious about someone who didn't have a strong background of family ties like my own. You know, the same values, the same way of looking at life. People don't realize how much excess baggage they can bring to a relationship, just because of things that happened to them as children."

Jason was scowling. "You're saying that a person has no control over his responses, Lori. I disagree."

She shook her head. "No. That's not what I meant. Besides, it's really only an abstract concept for us, isn't it, Jason? I mean, you live in one place and I live in another. I love my job teaching aerobics and fitness, and you're obviously quite attached to whatever it is you do."

"And if it wasn't like that?"

She looked into his eyes—eyes that mesmerized her every time she grew brave or foolish enough to stare into them. "I can't tell you," she said, "because I honestly don't know." A smile gently curled the corners of her mouth. "And from the reactions I've already had to you, Mr. Daniels, I suspect that's just as well."

"We could pretend this isn't a hopeless situation," he whispered, his breath lifting wisps of hair and brushing them against her cheek.

"Or, we could face what we do have and make the most of it," Lori countered.

Jason placed his hands on her bare shoulders and began stroking the sensitive hollow next to her collarbone with his thumbs.

She closed her eyes for a moment, stretching her neck and letting her head fall back until her hair swung free of her shoulders. "Umm. No fair."

"What's not fair?"

His look of total naïveté was so convincing, Lori would have been taken in if she hadn't recalled the fun he'd had teasing her about nice girls hanging around elevators, trying to pick up strange men.

"You know darned well what," she insisted. "I'm trying to have a philosophical discussion with you and you're distracting me."

"Me? What did I do?" Jason struggled to keep the smile off his face and lost. A wide grin made the tiny lines at the corners of his eyes crinkle delightfully.

Well, at least they had recaptured a lighter mood, Lori thought. The charmingly mysterious rogue was back and the pensive worrier was gone. For now.

She admitted to herself how difficult it would be to spend long periods of time with him and congratulated herself on her realization. The strain of trying to keep him happy would be dreadful, and judging from the way he had behaved up until now, perhaps impossible.

Yet she liked Jason. He had charm and a ready wit when he wasn't brooding over some real or imagined trouble. Thoughts of his confession of being a con man flashed through Lori's mind as she studied his handsome features.

I suppose he *could* be almost anything, she decided; a crook, a lawyer, an accomplished actor, even a normal businessman who took everything in life too seriously. Or he could be simply a lonely man whose disrupted childhood had made him skeptical of accepting friendship or affection, no matter how freely given, she added thoughtfully. Perhaps it would help if she could show him that he was safe with her, since once he went home, there would be no way they could hope to keep a close personal relationship alive.

Slowly, Lori lifted her gaze to his. "It would never work between us, Jason. I want you to admit that."

"I've only kissed you once," he said. "Don't you think you're getting a little ahead of yourself?"

"Twice," Lori retorted, "but who's counting?"

"When? I can't believe I missed it."

"Once lips, once cheek," Lori said. "In the kitchen."

He faked a scowl. "Cheeks don't count."

"Okay. Have it your way," she conceded. "The important thing is, I've made up my mind about us."

"And?" Jason's fingers continued to trace tiny circles on her shoulder. He fought to sustain his calm demeanor as he watched Lori's eyes grow wider, her lips parting in response to him.

"And I think we should lay down some ground rules."

"Why?"

Jason's voice made the hairs on the back of Lori's neck prickle and sent a shiver down her spine. She knew what he was doing to her; how he was breaking down her resistance with the subtle suggestions of his hands. And she also knew what she had to do before his touch and his closeness made her change her mind.

"Because I think we can be good friends if we don't get carried away and do something we're both sorry for," she said solemnly.

His jaw clenched. Damn it, she's right, Jason told himself. He held his breath, closed his eyes for an instant and fought the hardest battle of his life. He knew Lori wasn't anything like the other women in his life had been. Not like Monica. Lori was special. One of a kind. Vulnerable in spite of her sensible attitudes. And no amount of apology, later, could make up for a stupid mistake now.

Vicki had been right when she'd chided him about his hormones, Jason reflected. It had been his original intention to become Lori's friend, yet he'd found himself making another kind of overture toward her without thinking. There was no denying that what he was beginning to feel was wonderful, all right. The trick was going to be keeping his hands off the lovely Ms. Kendall until a more suitable time.

Lori smiled up at him. "Don't look so down in the dumps. We can still have a good time together."

His fingers had ceased their ministrations, and she saw the muscles in his jaw clench. As much as Lori wanted him to hold her in his arms, she knew the end result would be disaster for them both. With a tiny smile, she reached up and took his hands in hers. He didn't resist.

Before she could decide what else to say to him, he had nodded, pulled away from her and started for the door.

"I'd better be going, Lori. It's late."

Quietly, unprotestingly, she followed him onto the porch, picking up Muggsy to keep the little dog from dashing to the

Buick. When Jason paused at the foot of the stairs, she said softly, "Don't run away just because there's no right time or place for us, Jason."

He laughed dryly. "If there isn't, I'm a bigger fool than I thought." He reached the curb and turned back to her. "Speaking of time, when shall I pick you up tomorrow?"

Lori's breath caught in her throat. He still wanted to be with her, even after she'd spoken so plainly about their relationship! When he'd left the house so quickly, she'd assumed her talk of rules was driving him away for good. Joy filled her to overflowing.

"During the summer, we won't find an unoccupied place to spread a blanket unless we get there early," she said. "How about eight?"

Jason nodded. "You're not angry about tonight, are you?"

Gently, she said, "No. Of course not." When he stood, expectantly, she added, "Are you?"

He shook his head, looking at her thoughtfully. "No. You were right. I was out of line."

"But quite wonderful," Lori said.

"I'll bet you sounded like your grandmother just then."

With a chuckle, she agreed. "Probably." He climbed into the car. "Take care."

Waving, Jason started the engine, pulled away from the curb and was gone.

Surprised at how lonely she suddenly felt, Lori gave Muggsy a hug and went inside, promising herself that tomorrow would soon come and that Jason would return.

The trouble was, she missed him already. What was it going to be like for her when he left for good? she wondered.

A shiver shook her. Darned cold evenings, she grumbled. Even in the summer you need a sweater.

Low clouds masked the morning sun, telling Lori that the temperatures at the ocean would be cooler than usual, too

cold for the skimpy bikini and light cover-up she'd planned
to take, so she pulled on her favorite sweatshirt, an oversize
white one decorated with dancing bears in pink aerobic togs.
Not particularly sexy, but quite appropriate if she intended
to stick to her vow to treat Jason just as a friend. The red
bikini? Well, a girl needed to look attractive. Besides, it was
the only decent suit she owned.

To her assemblage of beach necessities she added another sweatshirt she hoped would be large enough for Jason,
should he need it. One without cute pictures. She held the
shirt close for a moment, thinking of him, then rolled it up
and shoved it into the large canvas tote she always took to
the beach.

A piece of toast and a cup of tea were all she could convince her stomach to tolerate. Pacing the floor, she waited.
Maybe Jason had changed his mind. Maybe he was only
being kind and trying to let her down gently. Why should
she believe his promise that he'd show up as scheduled when
they hardly knew each other?

Lori chewed her lower lip. Jason wouldn't lie to her. Of
that she was certain. He might withhold some information
about his life for personal reasons, but she knew he'd never
lie. He just wasn't that kind of man.

But what kind of man is he? she mused. He certainly
demonstrates gallantry in awkward situations, yet at the
same time he refuses to divulge enough about himself to let
me feel a part of his life.

Wandering from room to room, Lori absently stroked her
antique furniture and paused to appreciate the possessions
that gave her so much pleasure. She breathed deeply, con-
templatively. Possessions weren't all there was to life, she
reminded herself. Belonging was every bit as important.

The sound of a car caught her attention. Drawing aside
the lace curtains, she peeked out the window and felt her

heart leap into her throat. The green Buick was pulling to a stop!

Before Jason could get out and come to the door, Lori grabbed her bag and dashed outside, waving. "Hi!"

"Hello, yourself. Are you ready?"

"You bet." Jason reached across to open her door, and she tossed her bag into the back seat.

He looked past her. "Where's Muggsy?"

"Muggsy? You want the *dog* when you already have me?" Lori was in a teasing mood. "I warn you, he doesn't own a bikini."

"And you do?"

"You're darn tootin' I do. Red, yet." She climbed in and shut the door. "Besides, the beach is usually too hot for dogs and they're not allowed where I go."

"But, I could have sworn I saw dogs—" Jason stopped himself when Lori began to frown. Damn. He'd slipped again.

"You saw what? Have you been to the beach behind my back, Jason Daniels?"

"I never said I hadn't been there, did I? Now, are we taking Muggsy or not?"

"Nope. I took him in to be groomed early this morning, and Annette is going to pick him up if we're not home by three."

Jason looked aghast. "Not pink bows and fluff! Please, tell me you didn't do that to my little pal."

"Of course not. He'll come home looking as macho as ever."

"Whew! Thank goodness. The poor little guy is likely to have an identity crisis if you mess with his image."

"Speaking from experience, Mr. Daniels?"

"Wouldn't you like to know."

"As a matter of fact, yes, I would. I don't suppose you're ready to tell all, are you?"

Jason blessed her with his most charming smile. "Not unless you're ready to be bored to death."

"I'm willing to chance it," Lori said.

"Brave girl. A true daughter of the pioneers, facing annihilation at every turn with never-flinching courage."

Lori took a playful poke at him, and he ducked melodramatically. "Are you going to sit there all day arguing with me, or are we going to the beach?" she asked.

"The beach. Definitely the beach." Jason started the car. His smile widened. Lori's legs were smooth and tanned, as he knew they'd be, and they seemed to go on forever. Her feet were tucked into sandals. Her ankles were narrow, her calves shapely and her thighs disappeared beneath her sweatshirt just about the time his libido took off to soar into the blue summer sky.

"I certainly hope you have your bathing suit on under that sweatshirt," Jason said. "If not, you're liable to be arrested for indecent exposure."

"Don't you wish," Lori shot back. She tugged the garment lower on her hips, effectively hiding what there was of her bikini. "I'll leave you to imagine just what I *am* wearing till we get to the beach and see if it's warm enough to disrobe."

"It had better be," Jason said, still grinning as he drove. "Or I may faint from the strain of wondering what you look like under that tent you're wearing."

"You know darned well what I look like, Jason Daniels. Men have the knack of envisioning things like that."

"And women don't?" Jason raised one eyebrow. "You've never pictured me dressed in anything but this?" He looked down at his striped sport shirt, cotton slacks and running shoes.

Oh, boy, Lori thought, I sure left myself open to that one! The first time they'd met, she'd had lascivious thoughts and he knew it. He'd seen her blush and taunted her with misleading statements until she'd lost her cool and become a blithering fool. Denial, now, would only accentuate her embarrassment.

"Well..." Lori felt familiar warmth flowing to her cheeks. "Maybe."

"Uh-huh. I thought so. Well, I happen to have on a bathing suit, too, and I'm going to let *you* guess how *I* look." He glanced her way. "All I'll tell you is that it fits as well as it did when I was on the college swim team."

"Very impressive." Lori rolled her eyes. "I suppose now you'll tell me that you were the team captain."

"In my senior year. A real lady-killer, too."

"I'll bet."

Jason chuckled softly. "Never bet unless you're sure you're right, Lori."

"I don't need to bet. All I need to do is wait patiently and I'll get to see this magnificent physique of yours. Right?"

"Right. In all its splendor."

"You're modest, too, I see." It was all she could do to keep from giggling.

"Well, I'll leave that for you to decide. You're the fitness expert." He grinned broadly as he piloted the Buick through the light midmorning traffic. "I'm sure you can pretty well guess what you'll see."

"Hairy chest?" Lori asked.

"Yup."

"Narrow waist?"

"You bet."

"Great legs?"

"*I* think so." Jason began to chuckle. "So, eat your heart out, Ms. Kendall."

"I plan to. I also plan to pray for sunshine so I can make my own judgments."

Jason stopped at a traffic light. "While you're making decisions, you can tell me how we're getting to your favorite haunts. The Foothill freeway is just ahead."

"Right. Take that to the 605, then drop down to the 10 and it'll take us to the coast." Lori settled back against the velvet-upholstered seat. "I think it'll probably be too chilly to swim when we get there, so I want to show you the Santa Monica pier first. We can bum around, ride the carousel and eat hot dogs and frozen bananas till the sun comes out."

"Santa Monica?" Jason couldn't help the panic that crept into his voice. "Aren't there miles of other beaches all over the place?"

"Sure, but..." She frowned over at him. "What do you have against Santa Monica?"

"Nothing," Jason lied.

"Good. Then that's where we'll start. Okay?"

"Okay." Jason's hands closed tightly around the steering wheel. Of all the places for Lori to choose, why did it have to be Santa Monica? He knew probably two dozen Californians, not counting the other contestants at *Treasure Hunters*, and all but three of them lived on the beachfront in Santa Monica! Hell, *he* lived there.

Chapter Five

Jason parked in a lot below the famous wooden pier, dropped coins in the parking meter and followed Lori as she climbed the sand-covered concrete stairs to the boardwalk.

The enormous, two-story, rose-colored carousel house with its glassed archways and blue-trimmed windows dominated the scene, while rows of small shops and carnival games lined the outlying portions of the pier.

Lori, her canvas beach bag slung over one shoulder, took Jason by the hand, urging him along when he hesitated. Odors hinting of culinary delights intermingled with the fresh salt air, held close by the foggy atmosphere.

"Umm. Smell that ocean?"

He wrinkled up his nose. "Is *that* what I smell?"

"Come on. To look at you, you'd think you were scared of having fun."

"I'm not real fond of crowds. That's all."

"Then we chose the right time of day to come," Lori told him. "There'll be hundreds more people here as soon as the weather warms up."

"Terrific."

"I'll bet you got the good sportsmanship award in school," Lori said sarcastically.

He made a face. "And *I'll* bet you were one of those always peppy, cheerleader types. Am I right?"

"I should have left you at home and brought the dog, instead. He's better company."

"I don't bite," Jason said. "At least not as a rule."

"You don't smile, either." Lori tried to lead him farther down the boardwalk, but he balked.

"Can we go now?"

Lori stopped, hands on her hips, and faced him. "What's the matter with you? I thought you acted strangely a couple of times before, but this is ridiculous."

"I'd simply rather be swimming. That's all."

"Well, why didn't you say so?" Lori started back down the boardwalk swinging her bag. "I can skip eating and ride the carousel later. Come on. We'll go stake our claim to a place on the sand. Then you can pout all you want."

She noticed that Jason's pace immediately quickened. Trying to distract him, she pointed at surfers in brightly colored wet suits, paddling with their boards diagonally across the breakers, some of them riding dangerously close to the barnacle-covered pier pilings.

"I've always wanted to try that," Lori said.

"They're crazy." He lifted one eyebrow. "I thought you had better sense."

"Oh, I don't know. It looks exciting. Just like the *Treasure Hunters* auditions turned out to be." She eyed him quizzically. "Where's your sense of adventure?"

"I get plenty of adventure in my daily life without risking my neck for thrills."

"Oh? You mean in your capacity as a con man?"

Jason jumped the last eighteen inches down to the beach and held out his hand to help her. "Something like that."

Lori slipped off her sandals, took his hand and joined him. "I figured as much. Someday, you'll have to tell me why you bothered to try out for a game show when you're already so overburdened with excitement."

She pulled out the lightweight blanket she had tucked into her bag, chose a dry, fairly flat spot and spread it neatly. "There. We're home."

"Good." Jason sat down with his back to the pier, crossed his legs, turned up his shirt collar and put on mirrored sunglasses.

Lori began to laugh. "Who are you expecting? The Mafia?"

"That's probably funny in California, but you don't say things like that to a kid from Chicago's West Side."

"Sorry." Lori regarded him seriously. "You're not . . ."

"No. I'm not connected with the mob, if that's what you're asking."

She made a flamboyant gesture of relief, clutching her folded hands to her chest. "Whew. Thank goodness."

"That's what my mother said."

"Now, we're getting somewhere." Lori joined him on the blanket, folding her legs under her. "So, tell me about your mother. Does she live in Chicago, too?"

He nodded, breathing deeply. "My mother steadfastly refused to leave the old neighborhood. She says it's like a big family and in a way it is. People there know each other so well there are few secrets." He leaned back. "For instance, if you went to Julio's market on the corner of Chestnut and Dewitt and said, 'Give me the kind of cheese Mrs. Daniels always buys,' he could do it."

Jason pictured his mother at the worst time of the year, bundled in her brown wool coat, trudging through the late-winter slush to the market. He'd given her a fur, which she stubbornly refused to wear, claiming it was too ostentatious and insisting she'd be banned from her circle of friends if she "put on airs."

Lori noticed a faraway look in Jason's eyes and wondered how he could apparently miss a place so much when he'd be returning to it in a few days.

The waves washed up on the shore with hypnotic evenness, drawing Jason further into a meditative mood. The one thing he hated about his move to California was leaving his mother with no actual relatives close by. Everybody in the old neighborhood *did* know her. Still, she was so damn independent it would be difficult to tell for sure if she was all right, or if she needed anything, without actually being there to check up on her. Not that he couldn't fly to Illinois whenever he needed to.

A wave slid close to the edge of the blanket, then retreated beneath the next incoming breaker, leaving a line of frothy white bubbles on the sand. As Jason's eyes followed the path of the foam, he noticed a fiftyish matron in a floppy straw hat picking up broken bits of shell.

He stared. The closer she got, the more positive he was that she was 102B, the inquisitive, self-appointed greeting committee for the condo he'd recently moved into. Her name was Hastings, or Hawthorne, or some such thing. It didn't matter. She knew *him* and that was enough.

Jason stood, stripping off his glasses. "Come on, Lori. I'll race you to the water."

She hugged her knees. "Umm. Not me. It's still too cold. You may be used to the temperatures in Lake Michigan, but I'm not."

"Nonsense. After the first shock, you'll love it."

"After the first shock, I'll be frozen solid." She peered up at him. "I'll stay right here, thank you."

His shirt went first. Then his shoes and socks. As Jason reached for the buckle of his belt, Lori took an involuntary breath. Ooh, boy, she thought, if the rest of him matches what I can see already, I'm in deep trouble.

It did. Jason's waist was narrow, the dark hair on his upper body tapering to disappear beneath a sleek black swimsuit.

Jason glanced over his shoulder. Mrs. What's-her-name was getting closer by the minute. She'd stopped to talk to a family a scant thirty feet away, and it was only a matter of time before she got to Lori's blanket. If he left now and went into the surf alone there was no telling what the woman might say to Lori or how far he might have to swim to escape her eagle-eyed nosiness.

"Last chance to go quietly," Jason said.

"Nope. I'm waiting for the sun."

"I hate to tell you this," Jason said menacingly, "but in *my* neighborhood, the man is boss."

Lori scowled at him. "What century do you come from?"

"Some of my ancestors were Vikings," he said. "And the rest were Irish rebels. Our attitudes haven't changed much in the past twelve hundred years."

She rose to her feet, her hands on her hips. "Oh, they haven't? Well, *women* have, Mr. Daniels. Nobody bosses us around anymore."

His smile showed his straight white teeth. His eyes glistened. Without another word of warning, he scooped Lori up in his arms and strode across the damp sand toward the ocean.

Her warrior, she thought, clinging to his neck. Her paladin. Her dashing rogue with the flashing eyes and taut body. And he was carrying her off just as she had imagined he would. The only things missing were the cheers of his cohorts, the furrowed sails and dragon's-head bow of the Viking long ship, and the clashing broadswords and swift arrows of her defenders, to which Jason was, of course, impervious.

Jason was in the water up to his knees and starting to forge deeper into the incoming waves when Lori finally found her voice. "Put me down."

"No."

"I said, put me down. Now!" She mustered all the ire she could, knowing it was far too little to deter Jason Daniels from anything he wanted to do. She tried reasoning with him. "You'll get my sweatshirt wet, and it's all I have to keep me warm."

"I thought you craved adventure."

"I'm not suicidal!" Waves lapping against Jason's legs splashed up to smack Lori's bottom. With a yelp she hoisted herself higher and clung tightly to him. "Hey! That's cold."

"Shush. You'll attract attention."

"Good," she said loudly. "Maybe someone will rescue me."

"*I'm* rescuing you, Lori. Can't you tell?"

"Rescuing me from what?" Her voice rose in pitch until she was squeaking. Glancing past Jason's shoulder, she saw a nearby swimmer wave and give him a thumbs-up signal.

"From the lecherous surfers, of course," Jason said as he followed her line of sight.

Hugging him frantically, Lori pulled a face. "You just like to torture people. You Vikings are all alike."

He paused, braced himself, then jumped to ride up and over the swell as a breaker passed. "I thought you didn't believe me."

"I didn't," Lori said. "I thought all Norsemen had to be blond, but I'm rapidly changing my mind." The wave splashed, soaking the back of her sweatshirt and chilling her to the bone. "Ooow!"

"You're forgetting all those alliances with conquered maidens."

She made a wry face at him, then wondered if he had noticed or cared, since his gait didn't alter.

A quick glance at the shore showed Jason that 102B was shading her eyes with her hands and staring straight at him. Terrific. "Be quiet and behave yourself," he ordered.

"Make me." Lori was cold, miserable and growing more than a little angry at his aberrant behavior. "I'll bet you tortured bugs when you were a boy."

"Did not."

His adversary onshore was finally walking away, Jason noted. Good. A few more minutes, and he could safely carry Lori back to the comfort of her blanket and make the necessary apologies.

He gazed out to sea and his eyes widened in disbelief. Oh, God! He hadn't counted on nature's intervention in his scheme.

The approaching wave was enormous, curling and breaking earlier than the previous surf. He knew there was no way he could jump high enough to escape it and he was too far from shore to make it to the shallows in time. His only choice was to shield her with his own body and hope for the best. One thing was certain; the wave was going to hit and cover them, and Lori Kendall was going to yell her pretty head off.

Jason reacted instinctively, bracing himself, then drawing her attention. "Lori?"

She tilted her head back. "What do you—"

His lips came down hard on hers, taking her breath away and effectively silencing her screams as the icy salt water crashed over them.

Jason lost his balance but not his hold on Lori. Her response to him, in spite of her pretense of rage, was as thrilling as he knew it would be. The kiss he'd given her in the Hollywood parking lot was nothing compared to their marvelous joining beneath the breaker. Floating under the surface, he turned so she lay above him, sheltering her from the raspy sea bottom as the momentum of the water washed them shoreward.

Lori felt suspended in time and space, held firmly in the cocoon of his embrace. There was no one else but Jason and her. The whole world was theirs, made just for the two of them.

Bathed in the cradle of the sea, Lori drifted on her dreams, carried along by the unbelievable wonder of the moment. She was ecstatic. She was his. She was—drowning!

Fighting to breathe, Lori wrenched free and reached the surface first. Of all the crazy stunts!

Gasping, she struggled to stand. "You barbarian!"

Jason popped up beside her. "Me?"

"Yes, you!" She placed both hands on the top of his head before he could regain his balance and shoved him under.

"Hey!" This time, he backed away from her as he surfaced. "Some gratitude!"

"Gratitude? For what?" Lori was still sputtering, her eyes burning from the salt water.

Jason pushed back his wet hair with both hands. "For saving you, of course."

"You're crazy. The only thing I need saving from is you." Looking down at her soggy sweatshirt, Lori tried futilely to wring it out, gave up in disgust and began to make her way toward shore, trying her best to stamp her feet in spite of the thigh-deep water.

"Hey, wait! I did save you. I gave you mouth-to-mouth resuscitation in spite of being in great peril myself."

Lori squinted back at him. Her hair was dripping rivulets of water down her flushed cheeks, but she didn't care. "That wasn't how we did it in the first-aid class I had to pass to get my job."

He caught up to her and reached out to smooth her wet hair off her forehead. "It wasn't? Well, that's how we do it in Chicago."

Shoving his hand away, she scowled. "Stop that." She had expected the look on his face to reflect surprise, or anger, or even mock chagrin. Instead, what she saw in Jason's eyes could only be described as real anguish.

His smile was gone. "I'm sorry, Lori. Honestly I am."

She paused in her trek to shore. "Go on."

"It was a stupid move. I can see that now." He held out his hands in supplication. "Please, don't let it spoil our day?"

"No more tricks?" Lori was purposely scowling, making an effort to look irate, while Jason's expression was so contrite she knew she couldn't deny him forgiveness.

He shrugged. "Tricks? Me?"

"Yes, you, Jason Daniels," Lori said, finally giving in and smiling at him. She was rewarded by his look of relief. "Okay. The sun is beginning to peek out and warm things up. We'll go swimming for real, as soon as I get rid of these wet clothes, so I don't actually drown."

Jason followed her onto the beach and paused at the edge of the blanket with his back to the direction his neighbor had taken when she left the beach. "I could always resuscitate you again."

His grin was broad and Lori acknowledged to herself that he was the best-looking man around. "Right." She crossed her arms and reached for the hem of her sweatshirt.

"I'll do that for you." Covering her hands with his, he grasped the hem of the shirt, lifting the soggy dancing bears up and over Lori's head. In the split second it took to pull the shirt all the way off, he drew in his breath sharply.

She saw the stunned expression on his face and laughed. "You thought I was kidding about the red bikini, didn't you?"

"Well, no, I . . ."

"Uh-huh. That's what I thought. I sure hope you express yourself more clearly if you get to play *Treasure Hunters*."

Jason rolled her shirt into a tight ball. If he didn't hit the water again, soon, he was going to embarrass the hell out of himself. Thrusting her wet clothing at her, he turned on his heel and trotted back into the surf. It wasn't a cold shower, but it would have to do.

"Hey! Where are you going?"

"Swimming. Are you coming?"

She had already caught up to him and leaned around to look him in the eye. "You in a hurry?"

"You might say that."

"Well, what if I need further resuscitating?" Lori swore she could see his neck and cheeks darkening.

Waist-deep in water, Jason turned with a smile and a shake of his head. "I'm afraid we'll have to find a California lifeguard, then. The Chicago method of lifesaving is too hard on the hero."

"It's pretty hard on the victim, too," Lori said. "My heart is still pounding."

His eyes trailed over the part of her that was above the surf and he mumbled, "So I see."

"It's not polite to stare."

"Then don't wear that damn suit, again," he countered. "I am human, you know."

"That, I had noticed." Lori smiled up at him. It was no illusion. Jason Daniels was blushing. With a lighthearted laugh, she turned to the open ocean, timed her attack and plunged into the next swell as it crested.

She kicked and stroked hard, gaining a good head start on him, but her strength was no match for Jason's. He caught her. His arms were strong and reassuring, and she twisted within his embrace to face him while they both treaded water.

"At least you'll have to admit that *now* you've kissed me twice," she reminded him.

"Once," he contradicted, smiling. "Mouth-to-mouth resuscitation doesn't count, any more than cheeks do."

Lori ducked out of his grasp and swam away. She saw him grin broadly and start after her as she shouted back, "Liar!"

* * *

Lori was exhausted by the time she and Jason at last waded out of the surf. She reached into her beach bag, handing him a towel.

"Thanks." He wiped his face, slung the towel around his neck and flopped onto the blanket. "Whew! That was some workout."

"Yes." She joined him. "You definitely told the truth."

Jason felt his whole body tense. "About what?"

"The swim team." Lori leaned over and began to towel-dry her hair. "What did you think I meant, Chicago mouth-to-mouth?"

"Something like that." He started to rub the towel vigorously over his arms and shoulders. His mind had been wandering all morning and he still wasn't any closer to deciding what to do next about his relationship with Lori. One thing he *was* certain about, though. He wasn't going to kiss Lori Kendall again, under any circumstances, until he was free to be himself and tell her the truth. Not that he was being a gentleman, he admitted freely. He just didn't think he could go on kissing her and be sure he'd retain his sanity.

Jason chuckled to himself. Sanity? Hell, if he was sane he'd be at home alone, or at least out with a woman who wasn't so dangerous to his career. But, oh no, not him. He had to be attracted to a would-be contestant, the one class of human being totally off-limits to someone in his profession. Well, if McAlister wanted all his executives to experience the pitfalls of the job, he certainly wasn't going to be disappointed where Jason Daniels was concerned.

Lori was waving her hand in front of his eyes. "Hello in there. Anybody home?"

"Sorry."

"Do you often have out-of-body experiences?" she asked. "I've heard they're more common than most people think."

"More like out of mind." With a half smile, he offered his hand and helped her to her feet. "Come on. Let's go see that merry-go-round you told me about. I'll treat you to a ride."

"You have to ride with me. The carousel's an antique, and beautifully restored. Who knows, maybe you'll catch the brass ring."

"Win a prize, you mean?" His gaze traveled appreciatively over her. "I think I already have."

Lori laughed softly, averting her eyes to keep from blushing. "In the old days, the riders who managed to snare a brass ring while the carousel was in motion, could turn it in for a free ride."

His fingers clasped hers as they started to stroll slowly up the beach toward the boardwalk. "You know, honey, sometimes I feel like my whole life's been a free ride."

"How?"

Pensive, Jason paused, turning her to face him while he tucked stray wisps of her hair behind her ears. "Compared to most people, I had it pretty easy, I guess. In spite of my parents' divorce, my father provided very well for me, tuition to the best colleges and everything I needed for comfort."

"That's wonderful." Lori stared at the creases in his forehead. "Isn't it?"

He shrugged. "Yes. It would have been even nicer, though, if he'd been able to find the time to attend my graduation. After all he did pay for it."

Laying her hand on his arm, Lori said, "Oh, Jason. I'm so sorry. That must have hurt."

"No," he said quickly. "I didn't really expect him to come." Jason glanced back toward Lori's blanket. "Think it's safe to leave all your stuff?"

"Well..." It was clear to her that Jason had changed the subject on purpose. His childhood and youth had been so difficult she wondered how it was possible that he had emerged so strong, yet sensitive. Or perhaps he was that way because of his upbringing. Lori's heart went out to the young man still buried within Jason's current personality. She'd always had the unequivocal support of a big, loving family. She stared out to sea. How alone Jason must have felt.

"Hello," he said. "Earth to Lori." His fingers were snapping in front of her eyes. "Do you often have out-of-body experiences?"

Laughing, she grasped his hand to stop the snapping. "Okay, okay. I deserved that. I guess I daydream a bit, too."

"You do." Jason cocked his head toward their place on the sand. "The blanket and bag. Are they safe left there?"

"If I say yes, they're sure to be stolen," she told him, starting back. "Let's gather it all up and stow it in the car, then hit the pier and grab a hot dog."

"Haute cuisine, again? You'll spoil me. Are you sure our systems can tolerate all this fancy food?"

She spread her feet apart, hands on her hips. "If you're insinuating I don't feed you well enough, you're welcome to make other plans, Mr. Daniels. I thought you understood that this was the budget tour."

He held up his hands in a gesture of submission. "Okay. Don't get sore. I thought I remembered seeing a fresh-seafood stand when we first arrived, but if you want to poison that perfect body of yours with 'legendary tube steaks,' far be it from me to try to stop you."

Shaking the loose sand off the blanket, Lori rolled it up and stuffed it into her bag.

Jason was putting his shirt on when she tossed her soggy sweatshirt at him, hitting him squarely in the chest. "Hey! No fair. I didn't bring a change of clothes," he complained.

"You soaked it. You wring it out," Lori said, feigning anger. "I brought an extra one for you, but now I'm going to wear it, even if it is miles too big."

His eyebrows shot up in dismay. "And cover that bikini? You really know how to hurt a guy."

"I have no choice. That's all I brought and I'll begin to sunburn if I stay uncovered like this much longer."

"Your skin is fair." Jason dropped the sandy bears at his feet and stripped off his own shirt, handing it to Lori. "Here. Put this on and I'll go without till we head home. At least that way you can leave the front unbuttoned and the day won't be a total waste."

"Waste? I hardly know whether to be offended or flattered."

"Be flattered." He gave her his most disarming smile.

The shirt carried the sweet-spicy odor of Jason's aftershave and an added masculine aroma that made her skin tingle. She slipped it on and hugged it close. "Thanks."

His smile grew. "Thank *you*, Lori."

"For what?" she asked lightly, assuming he was still teasing her about the red bikini.

"For caring enough about me to bring an extra sweatshirt. That was very thoughtful." He busied himself wringing water from her wet clothing.

"You're welcome." Touched by his candor, yet unsure whether or not to address his feelings directly, Lori picked up their damp towels and wrapped them together as she watched him hoist her beach bag. Jason's moment of frankness seemed to have passed, so she turned to less serious conversation. "We tour guides try to think of everything."

"Next stop?" Jason asked, making sure there was a cheerful lilt to his voice.

"The car, then that seafood place you mentioned. Now that I think about it, I'm starved."

"Me, too." Jason took her hand. Her skin was warm, just a bit sandy and incredibly soft. The warmth of the summer sun was reflected in her eyes and her hair was burnished copper, surrounded by a golden halo of light.

He squeezed her fingers more tightly. In a few days they'd be called to the studio and his real trials would begin. Jason's jaw clenched. It was too soon. He'd had too little time. Lori liked him, he knew, but he could hardly expect her to understand why he'd lied.

"You're getting serious again," she warned. "I do wish you'd tell me what's bothering you."

He released her hand and put his arm around her shoulders, pulling her close. "I will, honey. I promise. As soon as possible, I'll level with you."

Looking up at him, she couldn't help feeling at a loss. "Will you answer one question?"

"If I can."

"Is your secret bad? I mean, is it something that can hurt you?"

"Perhaps." Jason set her beach bag on the ground, turned and placed both hands lightly on her shoulders. "But I don't want you to worry about it. All I want you to think about is what a great time we're having." And get to know me so you'll trust me no matter what, he added silently.

Lori stared at him, trying to decipher his perplexing expression. "Please, let me help. Whatever it is, surely it would be better to face it with a friend."

He shook his head sadly. "I'm sorry, Lori. This is something I have to deal with alone." Placing a kiss on her forehead, Jason picked up the bag, took her hand and led her toward the parking lot.

By the time dusk fell, they'd sorted out their clothing and Jason had finally agreed it was time Lori warmed up in the extra sweatshirt.

Lori drew the oversize garment closer to her body and leaned back against the car seat as the Buick pulled to a stop in front of her house. "What a lovely day. Thank you, Jason."

He shut off the ignition. "It was fun, wasn't it? I haven't loosened up and acted like a kid for a long time." He chuckled. "Remember those teenagers who kept staring at us?"

"Small wonder! You were trying to get on the carousel horse I was riding. I thought the attendant was going to boot us both off." A shiver went through her as she recalled the warmth and strength he had radiated, the muscles on his bare arms flexing effortlessly when he'd hoisted his body up beside hers.

"Did you, or did you not, tell me I had to ride *with* you? Huh? Whose fault is it that we made a spectacle of ourselves?" He leaned closer. "You're the tour guide, remember? I was just following orders."

Lori looked into his laughing eyes and felt her heart melt. This was the man she could supposedly see with impunity because he was going away. This was the man she didn't have to fear growing close to because his time in her life was so limited. She blinked to try to clear her thoughts. This was the man she had a whopping schoolgirl crush on already, and they'd only met two days ago!

"I guess I should have told you, I'm an unlicensed tourist service, Mr. Daniels. Sort of a fly-by-night operation, not to be relied on for accurate information as to the customs of the natives."

"Unreliable but charming," he said quietly.

Well, sitting here staring at her wasn't going to help their situation, Jason told himself. Not that he had the smallest idea as to what would. The more time he spent with Lori, the worse he felt about deceiving her.

Thoroughly disgusted with himself, he climbed out of the Buick, dusting the errant grains of sand off his slacks. In his haste to see Lori again, he hadn't carefully thought out his wardrobe for their trip to the beach. Cursing under his breath, he acknowledged that he had no one but himself to blame for the fact that he had sand in some pretty uncomfortable places.

He unlocked the trunk and gathered up Lori's possessions. "Shall I carry all this for you?"

"Yes, if you don't mind," Lori said, joining him. "Would you like to come in for a while?"

Jason nodded as he lifted her bag. "And what about tomorrow?" He followed her up the walk and stood at the foot of the stone steps while she fished for her house key.

"Tomorrow? Oh! I'd like that. Where shall we go?"

Before she could fit her key into the lock, the door was thrust open. Lori jumped aside with an unintelligible cry. "Aah!"

Muggsy shot by, followed by a breathless Annette. "Geezlouise! Where have you been, Lori?" Her eyes darted to Jason and back to her friend. "Never mind. I don't want to know. My heart couldn't take another shock."

"Annette, for heaven's sake. Calm down and tell me what's wrong. Is Muggsy all right? Did the groomer have trouble with him?"

"Muggsy? Forget the dog. We have plans to make! Clothes to buy!" Annette took Lori by the arm and dragged her into the house.

Muggsy found Jason, jumped up and down at his feet and escorted him into the living room.

"Shall I leave this wet, sandy stuff by the door or take it into the kitchen?" Jason asked.

Lori spun back to him for an instant before Annette had time to object. "The bathroom, please. You know where it is."

Annette grasped both of Lori's shoulders. "He does?" She shook her head vigorously. "Never mind. That's not important. Listen to me, will you? Simone from *Treasure Hunters* phoned my house this afternoon. I have an interview with the producer!"

Lori hugged her. "That's great! I'm so happy for you."
She turned to seek out Jason. "Isn't that wonderful?"

He stepped back into the room, his hair freshly combed,
his expression bland. "Yeah. Nice."

"Nice!" Annette stared at him. "Nice? Wait till you hear
the rest of it." She held Lori at arm's length. "I came back
here with Muggsy about three o'clock, and *your* phone was
ringing. I let it go as long as I could, but the suspense was
killing me, so I answered it." She waited, staring at Lori
expectantly.

Slowly the light dawned. Lori gasped. "Me, too?"

"Yeah! Isn't it great? They want us both!"

Lori had momentarily ignored Jason. Now, she found
him standing apart, his hands thrust into his pockets, his
shoulders slumped. "Oh, I can't do it, Annette. I already
have plans. I'm sorry."

"Can't do it? You have to do it. I already accepted for
you."

"You what?"

"Well, I didn't know what to say, and I didn't want to
mess things up, so I pretended I was you. They want us in
Hollywood tomorrow morning."

"So soon?" Lori looked quickly from Jason to Annette
and back again. Life was often not fair, but this was the first
time she could recall it being downright heartless. She left
Annette and walked slowly over to Jason.

"It'll be okay," he said. The nightmare was beginning.

"But we were going to make new plans. You have so little time."

With a deep sigh, he shook his head. "Don't worry. I
know everything will turn out all right." He shot a wry smile
at Annette. "Congratulations."

"Thanks. Too bad we couldn't *all* be chosen," the frizzy
blonde said magnanimously.

As Jason started toward the door he looked back over his
shoulder at her. "Maybe we were. You never know."

Lori followed him out onto the porch. "I wish it could be true, Jason."

"How do you know it isn't?"

"It's too farfetched. I mean, consider the odds. Of all the people who tried out, why should the three of us be picked?"

He was leaning against the newel post at the edge of her porch railing. "Why not? We're all intelligent. Maybe they're looking for a cross-section. You know, one mod California type like Annette, one middle-America type like me and . . ." Warm color suffused his face.

"And? How do you picture me, Jason?"

"I'm afraid I'm not able to be objective about you anymore, Lori."

"Is that so bad?"

"No." Jason stepped closer to her, folded her in his embrace and pulled her against him.

Lori laid her cheek on his chest. She could feel the rapid thudding of his heart through the thin fabric of his shirt and sense the tension in his body as she slipped her arms around his waist and clung to him.

"I want you to know I think you're doing the right thing in sticking by Annette," he whispered against her hair.

"You know I'd rather be with you while I can, don't you?"

He nodded. "Yes. I also know you're the kind of person who's loyal to her friends, who honors her commitments." He placed a light kiss on the top of her head. "Don't ever be sorry about being like that. It's pretty unusual these days."

Lori fought the tears filling her eyes and pressed her face against him. It wouldn't do for him to see her crying. She didn't want his memory of her clouded by sadness.

"I'm glad we met, Jason. You're a very special man. When you get back to Chicago, I hope you'll think of me once in a while."

Slowly he released her, held her at arm's length and tilted up her chin to look into her eyes. "Not once in a while, Lori. All the time. Every day." A slight smile lifted the corners of his mouth. "And every night."

Lori saw him lean his head back, close his eyes and sigh. It was obvious he cared for her, too, and their parting was affecting him deeply. How selfish she had been to imagine that she would be more lonely than Jason when he left.

She raised her hand and let her fingers trail gently down his cheek, savoring the feel of his skin, the slight stubble emerging on his jaw. She heard him moan as his arms closed around her.

"Oh, Lori."

Standing on tiptoe, she touched her lips to his. Warm and supple, his mouth claimed hers with a tender passion that enveloped her in a swirling vortex of exploding emotions. It was like being beneath the waves with him again, tossed and turned, yet safe within the circle of his embrace. Wrapping her arms around his neck, she nestled closer.

Jason's breathing grew ragged. He'd promised himself this wouldn't happen, yet her caress had ignited a fire in him he was powerless to deny. He had to touch her, to hold her tight, if only for a moment.

Lori felt him shudder, then he reached for the hem of her shirt. His hand barely brushed the curve of her hips, coming to rest possessively in the small of her bare back. He pulled her against him, leaving no doubt as to the urgency of his need. She parted her lips, responding to the press of his and welcomed the intrusion of his tongue.

He told himself it was wrong to want her as he did. It wasn't fair to her. Until Lori knew what he was doing in California, he had no right to accept her affection, no matter how intense their emotional bond became.

One last time, Jason twisted his mouth hungrily against Lori's, then abruptly broke away. "I have to go."

"I understand." But she didn't. Why couldn't he stay and spend the rest of the evening with her? What was so urgent that he had to leave? He'd told her he thought she was doing the right thing by going back to the quiz show with Annette, so what was wrong?

Jason started down the steps to his car.

"Wait." Lori touched his shoulder.

"Lori, I..." The look in her eyes was devastating, reaching deep into his soul. He'd already hurt her, just by showing her how much he cared, and he hated everything about his profession for the first time since he'd begun it.

Standing one step above him, Lori stared straight into his eyes. The intensity she saw there convinced her Jason didn't want to go, any more than she wanted him to. Boldly she lowered her lips to his, claiming them with abandon.

His response was as she knew it would be, immediate and thrilling. Lori didn't know why he was fighting his natural urges toward her, but she did know that he was a strong man. The force of his willpower would eventually triumph over the yearnings of his body.

With a sigh that shook her whole body, she gave herself over to the magic of Jason's kiss and the urgency of what might well be their last moments together.

Chapter Six

Is he gone?" Annette asked.

"Yes." Lori let herself sink slowly into the stack of floor pillows. "For good, I imagine."

Annette joined her. "Hey, I'm really sorry. I hope it wasn't anything I did."

"No." Lori crossed her legs to cradle Muggsy as he made himself at home in her lap. Ruffling the little dog's silky fur, she sighed.

"'Course, it never would have worked between you two, anyway."

"I know. Chicago's awfully far to go for a date."

Annette stretched out, staring at the ceiling. "Oh, I don't mean that." She paused, raising herself on one elbow to look at Lori. "It was something else. There's just something funny about him."

"Are you jealous?"

"Maybe. I don't know. He's certainly good-looking enough. Don't you love that little notch in his chin?"

Lori shrugged and smiled. "You noticed?"

"Oh, yes. I may like my men a lot funkier, but if I did ever choose a three-piece-suit executive type, Jason Daniels would be him."

"That's funny," Lori said, rolling over and spilling Muggsy onto the floor. "You and I never saw him dressed that way, but I got the same impression about him."

The furry dog dashed under the table, found his favorite toy and brought it to Lori. Obligingly she pitched it across the room while she talked. "Why do you suppose we both thought that?"

"I don't know. You went out with him. What did he tell you?"

"Not much." Lori took the toy from Muggsy and threw it again. "He was pretty secretive."

"Bad sign." Annette's forehead furrowed.

"Yeah, that's what I thought at first. But after I'd been with him awhile, I forgot how little I knew about him and just enjoyed myself." She threw Muggsy's toy onto the couch to confuse him and end the game. "Jason really is a marvelous man. I can't remember when I've had that much fun or been more comfortable with anyone."

"Uh-oh. Do I detect heart palpitations and some serious heavy breathing here?"

Lori's memories of Jason's last kisses flooded her mind, bringing her pleasure with astonishing swiftness. "Don't be ridiculous."

"Am I being ridiculous?" Annette leaned closer to Lori. "Or are you falling for the guy and too stubborn to admit it?"

"Annette!"

"Don't 'Annette' me, Lori Kendall. I've known you since high school and every man you've started to get serious about has had some minor fault that you've sworn kept you from marrying him."

"Minor fault? What about George?"

"Okay. So there was one true stinker." Annette made a pouting face. "It's still time you got in touch with your feelings, listened to your heart and let it lead you into...whatever."

"Like you and Sam?"

"Bad choice of examples. Sam forgot to mention he was married."

"See?" Lori stood and paced the floor with Annette right behind her.

"Is Jason married?"

"No. At least he said he wasn't." She turned to face her friend. "And I believe him. He's not the kind of man who'd lie about that."

Annette spread her hands wide, palms up. "So? What's the problem? Arrange to see him after we're done with the TV show." She snapped her fingers. "Hey! You could probably get him into the audience and he could watch us play."

Lori brightened. "Do you think so?"

"Sure. I talked to a lady who'd been on a game show before and she said each contestant got to invite guests."

"Oh, that would be..." The animation went out of Lori like helium escaping from a punctured balloon. "I can't."

"Why not? Still waiting for Mr. Perfect?"

Lori shook her head. "That's not it."

Exasperated, Annette took her by the shoulders. "Then why?"

"I didn't get his number," Lori said flatly. "I have no idea how to reach him."

All the way home, Jason rehearsed the story he'd have to tell Lori. Just a few more days, he reminded himself. Just a few more days and he could confess everything and throw himself on her mercy.

He'd traded the Buick for his red Ferrari by the time he reached the gate of his condominium complex. Whizzing around the narrow inner courtyard, he pulled up in front of his private garage, pushed the control button and waited impatiently for the overhead door to lift. His fist hit the steering wheel. Damn slow door. Poor Lori thought he'd left her for good and he didn't want her to suffer one extra moment because of him.

The thought of her misty eyes and the valiant effort she'd made to bid him a cheerful goodbye wrenched at his gut. He'd been forced to hurt the one woman he wanted most to protect and care for.

Screeching into the garage, he bolted for his apartment, driven by the memory of Lori's pain.

Jason tossed his keys on the glass-topped table by his front door, grabbed the phone and dialed. It was Annette, not Lori, who answered.

"This is Jason Daniels. Is Lori there?" He held his breath.

"Whoa! Hang on. I'll get her." Annette dropped the receiver and dashed to the bathroom. "Lori! Telephone!"

"Take a message. I'm in the shower."

"It's Mr. Wonderful, stupid. Grab a towel and get out here!" Annette turned and jogged back to the phone. "Are you still there?"

"Yes."

"Good. Don't go away. She's coming."

He chuckled. "Okay. I promise I won't hang up. Now pull yourself together and save some of that energy for the game-show interview."

"Yeah. Thanks." Lori arrived, and Annette handed her the receiver.

"Hi."

"Hi. Are you all right?"

Lori felt her knees growing wobbly. She started to answer with the standard, "I'm fine," then changed her mind. "Not really. After you left, it occurred to me I had no way to reach you in case we finished *Treasure Hunters* before you flew home." She took a deep breath and sat down on the arm of the couch. "I felt really stupid for not thinking to ask where you're staying."

His voice was low and his words were spoken with deliberation. "I'm sorry, Lori. That's my fault. I should have told you I intended to call you every day to ask how the show was going."

"Annette says we may be able to get you into the audience."

"That won't be necessary."

"Why?" Lori's fingers were turning white from her nervous grip on the towel. "Can't you come?"

"No, no. It's not that," Jason said. "I've also received word that I've been recalled, so I'll see you there tomorrow." His fist was clenched, his stomach churning.

Lori's mouth dropped open. "You're kidding!"

"Not at all." It was good to hear her enthusiasm. The only thing missing was the feel of her pliant body nestled in his arms, the excitement he knew was dancing in her eyes.

"Oh, Jason, I'm so glad."

"So am I." He wasn't ready to field any more of her questions, so he simply said, "I'll see you soon. All right?"

"Of course, but—"

"Until tomorrow then. Sleep tight."

Lori heard the phone click as he hung up.

"Did you get his number?" Annette asked.

"No." Lori pulled a face. "But I'm beginning to think he's got *my* number, in more ways than one."

She padded back to the bathroom, turned on the shower and stepped beneath the stinging spray. Jason hadn't told her a thing more, except that he'd see her again. Well, she reasoned, at least she had that to look forward to.

Lori lifted her face into the cascading water. She knew she should be thankful for the promise of tomorrow, but tomorrow was only one day out of a lifetime. Seeing Jason again would almost be a cruel trick of fate.

Her tears began to flow, mixing with the water washing over her. Annette was right, Lori finally admitted. She *was* falling for Jason Daniels.

With a sniffle she spoke to the emptiness of the room. "I don't love him. I don't. I can't. It's impossible."

In a flash, her words to Jason as she swam away from his playful embrace echoed in her heart. "Liar."

Lori picked up Annette at 9:15 sharp. Fluffing her hair and lugging a tote that Lori was certain contained enough makeup to accommodate the entire female population of Hollywood, Annette hurried to the car.

She jumped in and slammed the door. "Hi."

"Hi."

Her mouth dropped open in shocked disbelief. "The silk," Annette wailed, "I told you to wear the turquoise silk! You can't go on TV in that. What happened?"

"I feel better in chambray," Lori said. "Besides, the weatherman predicted temperatures in the nineties today. Do you know how hot I'd be in silk?"

"That's the idea," Annette declared. "Hot, as in sexy, as in out to impress Mr. Wonderful." She rolled her eyes. "I don't believe you, Lori Kendall."

"I do wish you'd quit calling Jason Mr. Wonderful." She adjusted the drawstring neckline of her white eyelet blouse, smoothed the soft gathers of her dusky blue skirt and pulled into traffic.

Annette slumped down in the seat. "You're trying to get yourself thrown out, aren't you?"

"Nonsense. This outfit is casual, but just as nice as yours." She laughed softly. "And there's a lot more of it."

Wriggling her hips, Annette eased her skirt down another inch. It still fell eight inches above her knees. "Did you see the peekaboo back when I got in the car? I must have looked at a hundred dresses before I found one that was right for me."

```
***********************************************************
*  You may have already won a lifetime of cash payments *
*  totaling up to $1,000,000.00!  Play our Sweepstakes  *
*  Game--Here's how it works...                         *
***********************************************************
```

Each of the first three tickets has a unique Sweepstakes number.
If your Sweepstakes numbers match any of the winning numbers
selected by our computer, you could win the amount shown under
the gold rub-off on that ticket.

Using an eraser, rub off the gold boxes on tickets #1-3 to
reveal how much each ticket could be worth if it is a winning
ticket. You must return the <u>entire</u> card to be eligible. (See
official rules in the back of this book for details.)

At the same time you play your tickets for big cash prizes,
Silhouette also invites you to participate in a special trial of
our Reader Service by accepting one or more FREE book(s) from
Silhouette Romance.™ To request your free book(s), just rub off
the gold box on ticket #4 to reveal how many free book(s) you
will receive.

When you receive your free book(s), we hope you'll enjoy them
and want to see more. So unless we hear from you, every month
we'll send you 6 additional Silhouette Romance™novels. Each
book is yours to keep for only $2.25* each. There are <u>no</u>
additional charges for shipping and handling and of course, you
may cancel Reader Service privileges at any time by marking
"cancel" on your shipping statement or returning an unopened
shipment of books to us at our expense. Either way your
shipments will stop. You'll receive no more books; you'll have
no further obligation.

Plus--you get a FREE MYSTERY GIFT!

If you return your game card with **all four gold boxes** rubbed
off, you will also receive a FREE Mystery Gift. It's your
immediate reward for sampling your free book(s), **and** it's yours
to keep no matter what you decide.

P.S.

Remember, the first set of one or more book(s) is FREE. So rub
off the gold box on ticket #4 and return the entire sheet of
tickets today!

*Terms and prices subject to change without notice.
 Sales taxes applicable in New York and Iowa.

"GIVE YOUR HEART TO SILHOUETTE" SWEEPSTAKES

DETACH HERE AND RETURN ENTIRE SHEET OF TICKETS NOW!

#1 $1,000,000.00
Rub off to reveal potential value if this is a winning ticket: ▶

UNIQUE SWEEPSTAKES NUMBER: 6A 577527

#2 $1,000,000.00
Rub off to reveal potential value if this is a winning ticket: ▶

UNIQUE SWEEPSTAKES NUMBER: 7A 579512

#3 $1,000,000.00
Rub off to reveal potential value if this is a winning ticket: ▶

UNIQUE SWEEPSTAKES NUMBER: 8A 577178

#4 ONE OR MORE FREE BOOKS

HOW MANY FREE BOOKS?
Rub off to reveal number of free books you will receive ▶

1672765559

Yes! Enter my sweepstakes numbers in the Sweepstakes and let me know if I've won a cash prize. If gold box on ticket #4 is rubbed off, I will also receive one or more Silhouette Romance novels as a FREE tryout of the Reader Service, along with a FREE Mystery Gift as explained on the opposite page.   215 CIS HAX8

NAME _____

ADDRESS _____ APT. _____

CITY _____ STATE _____ ZIP CODE _____

Offer not valid to current Silhouette Romance subscribers. All orders subject to approval.   PRINTED IN U.S.A.

DON'T FORGET...

... Return this card today with ticket #4 rubbed off, and receive 4 free books and a free mystery gift.

... You will receive books well before they're available in stores.

... No obligation to buy. You can cancel at any time by writing "cancel" on your statement or returning an unopened shipment to us at our cost.

BUSINESS REPLY CARD

First Class   Permit No. 717   Buffalo, NY

Postage will be paid by addressee

Silhouette Reader Service ™

MILLION DOLLAR SWEEPSTAKES

901 Fuhrmann Blvd.
P.O. Box 1867
Buffalo, N.Y. 14240-9952

NO POSTAGE
NECESSARY
IF MAILED
IN THE
UNITED STATES

Lori smiled over at her. "I'm glad. Really I am. And I swear I'm not trying to get out of competing. You're forgetting, Jason will be there, too."

"I may have forgotten about him, but it sounds as if you haven't."

"Yeah." Raising her eyebrows, Lori glanced over at her friend. "Only I don't know what to do about it. I keep reminding myself he's leaving."

"So? Pretend he isn't."

"And make plans that can never be fulfilled? That's crazy."

"Okay. Have it your way."

Lori pulled a face. "At least I haven't had the likes of your friend, Sam, around to mess up my life."

"You haven't had anybody around to mess up anything." Annette patted Lori's arm. "Don't you think it's time you took a few chances?"

"I prefer better odds, I'm afraid."

Annette shook her head. "I don't know about the odds part," she said, "but I've suspected for a long time that you're afraid."

"I didn't mean it like that," Lori protested.

"Maybe not. At least not consciously. But you might want to give the idea some thought. You could do worse than to fall in love with Jason Daniels."

Lori's head snapped around. "Who said anything about love?"

The producer was younger than Lori had expected him to be. His attitude was one of withdrawn complacency, yet she was certain his small, dark eyes didn't miss a thing that went on in the room. His alertness and expression reminded her of Muggsy. Except, she mused, the producer's company manners were much better. He hadn't jumped up on the furniture or barked once since she'd arrived.

Jason entered the room after everyone else was seated. He was so well dressed that Lori did a double take.

"Ooh, wow," Annette whispered. "Will you look at that?"

"I am looking. That must be the fancy three-piece suit we both assumed he usually wore."

"Uh-huh. Some looker, isn't he?"

Lori elbowed her. "Shush. He'll hear you."

"You shush. Here comes Vicki."

"Good morning," Vicki said, seating herself on a table by the door and handing a stack of yellow cards to the producer. With a stiff smile, she began to instruct the group on what would be expected of them and how they could best deliver a concise oral introduction of themselves.

Lori listened intently, silently rehearsing what she intended to say when it was her turn.

After several people had already spoken Vicki finally smiled at Lori. "Now, tell us about yourself."

"I'm Lori Kendall from Monrovia, California. I teach yoga and aerobics and test clients for overall fitness." She thought she sounded self-assured, but wondered if her life lacked the glamour and excitement some of the other contestants had described since she didn't jump out of airplanes, write novels or work for any carefully unnamed major corporation.

Annette stammered a little, managing to struggle through with the help of a pat on the arm from Lori. "My Lord," she whispered after it was over. "You'd think I'd never introduced myself before!"

"You did fine." Lori was waiting anxiously for Jason's turn. Maybe he'd divulge something she didn't already know.

Jason delivered his speech as smoothly as a professional actor. "I'm Jason Daniels," he said, his voice deep and resonant. "My hometown is Chicago and I'm out here on the West Coast enjoying the sights." His eyes left Vicki to dwell for long seconds on Lori Kendall.

Lori met his gaze boldly. She thought she detected a slight loss of poise, a brief flash of intimacy, before he regained his composure. It seemed, no matter what the external pressures, Jason was able to carry on as if he were talking to a roomful of friends instead of trying out for a television producer. What experiences had he had, she wondered, to give him such magnificent aplomb?

"Did you see the look he gave you?" Annette asked.

"How could I miss it?"

"What're you going to do about it?"

"Oh, I guess I'll dash across the room, throw myself into his lap and tear off his clothes. How's that sound?" Lori chuckled at Annette's astonished expression. "Only joking."

"Well, stop kidding around," Annette said. "I've just had an awful thought."

Lori frowned. "What's wrong?"

"Look at the people in this room. I only recognize a few."

"So what?" Lori glanced at the eager faces.

"So, don't you get it? We can't all play. I figured we had it made when we got the call to come back, but it's evident we're in another elimination contest." Annette sat up straighter, squared her shoulders and displayed the most plastic smile Lori had ever seen.

"You took the call," Lori reminded Annette. "Didn't you ask?"

Annette's "No," was almost a sob.

Lori bit her lower lip. "I wish I could ask Jason. He'd know." She thought for a moment. "You said, interview, and Jason said he'd been recalled. That doesn't sound like we're home free, yet."

"I know. Quick! Smile! They're looking us over."

The best way for her to conjure up a feeling of genuine joy, Lori reasoned, was to look at Jason, so she treated herself to a long, assessing stare. He nodded and smiled back.

A sudden thought struck her. What if she was chosen and he wasn't? What would she do then? Lori put the disturbing idea out of her mind as best she could and busied herself studying Vicki. The older woman had ceased to remind Lori of Mrs. Fensterwald. Instead, she resembled a picky supermarket customer, shopping for the choicest morsels.

"I feel like a piece of meat," Lori whispered. "Look how seriously she's taking all this."

"And you don't? Geez-louise, my whole life is flashing before my eyes!" Annette leaned closer. "Smile wider, will you? She's pointing at us."

"If I smile any wider, my cheeks will cramp. My teeth are already dry." Lori ignored the sour look she got from her friend. As far as Lori was concerned, joking was the best way to lift the pressure and also take her mind off Jason Daniels. If that was possible.

She chanced another short peek at him, feeling her pulse accelerate immediately. One thing was for sure, she promised herself resolutely, he wasn't riding off into the sunset and getting away from her today. No, sir. Not again. She was tired of being kept in the dark.

Annette grabbed Lori's hand as Vicki got to her feet. The producer slipped quietly out the door, leaving Vicki standing alone in the center of the room, holding a small number of cards.

"We want to thank all of you for coming," Vicki said. "I'll call nine names. The rest of you may go for now. If you haven't heard from us in three months, you can assume you won't."

Lori held tightly to Annette.

"John, Alan, Larry, Jean, Annette..."

Annette launched herself into the air, shouting.

Before Lori could pull her back Vicki went on. "Lori, Jason..."

Casting aside any thought of polite, refined behavior, Lori joined in the wild celebration. Nine new contestants jumped, squealed and patted each other on the back, while the losers departed silently.

"I can't believe it!" Lori said breathlessly.

"I can." Jason's voice made the hairs on the back of her neck stand up and electricity flow all the way to the ends of her fingers and toes.

"Oh, Jason!" Turning, Lori threw her arms around him. His business suit made no difference in how he felt against her or in the marvelous way his arms wrapped around her. Reveling in her happiness at having him near, she kissed him.

"Not here," he warned. "Later."

Subdued, Lori let him go and stepped away. There was so much bedlam around them she doubted anyone had noticed what she'd done. Or cared. So what was Jason trying to do, pretend he didn't know her? If she ever figured him out, ever made sense out of his moods and actions, she'd give herself a medal, she decided.

Simone entered the room. "Okay. Party time is over. Everybody sit down, and I'll explain the rules."

Jason took Lori's elbow, seeing to it that she chose the chair next to his. Every plan he'd made so far that day had gone awry, and he wasn't about to relinquish the one bright spot in his trying morning: the chance to be near Lori.

Relaxing was impossible, Jason found. He could feel her warmth through his jacket, and when she smiled at him, he wondered if the quaking in his abdomen was visible.

He fidgeted. The first sight of her when he'd arrived had been exciting, yes, but when her whole countenance had become glowingly beautiful the moment their eyes met, Jason had wondered if he was going to make it across the room and into an empty chair. She took his breath away!

Imperceptibly Lori leaned closer to him. "I was afraid you weren't coming."

"So was I," he whispered. "It's been a hell of a morning."

"What happened?"

"A problem with the car." He'd been so overwrought about deceiving Lori he'd forgotten to reserve the Buick. California Rentals was unable to find another one on short notice, so he'd opted to keep his Ferrari and worry about explaining it later.

"How did you get here?"

"I'm driving a car that belongs to a guy who used to work in Chicago." True, but necessarily misleading. Jason congratulated himself on his choice of words.

Lori searched his face. "You have friends out here?"

He nodded as Simone dropped a bulky envelope in his lap and moved on to do the same to the other contestants. "Okay, you two. No fraternizing. We've got work ahead of us."

Blinking to clear her jumbled thoughts, Lori picked up the envelope. There was something wrong with Jason's story. He seemed too uneasy for his nervousness to be simply a case of quiz-show jitters. She glanced sideways at him while she extracted the contents of her envelope.

"The pink sheet is a map to the studio," Simone said. "It tells you about freeway access, street address and preferred parking. When you drive up to the guard house, give your name and tell them you've come to play *Treasure Hunters*."

She lifted a blue sheet. "Here are the dates for taping and some simple rules. You'll meet me under the white awning at the southwest entrance to Affiliated Broadcasting at the time listed. From the moment you pass the guard house, you're to speak to no one." She paused. "Is that clear?"

Lori's eyes widened. "Why?"

"Because you'll be watched every second, Lori. If you're seen talking to anyone other than me, Vicki, or the people in this room, you'll be out of the game." She smiled benevolently. "It's for your own protection. There's a special enforcement department at all the networks that's in charge of keeping everyone honest. Believe me, they take their jobs seriously."

Annette couldn't keep still. "You mean we'll be like prisoners? We can't even say hello?"

Clucking and shaking her head, Simone said, "No. As a matter of fact, some of the technicians and production people think it's funny to try to get contestants to break the rules. They'll do all kinds of silly things to disrupt your chances. It's a game to them."

"That's not fair," Annette exclaimed, and others murmured their agreement.

"But that is how it is," Simone said flatly. "Now, shall we get on with this?" Shuffling through the papers, she held up a legal-size sheet. "Find this one and read it before you sign. It's a contract stating you will abide by all the rules and swearing you have no connection with either Affiliated Broadcasting or its employees."

Quickly Lori scanned the contract. It was straightforward and blunt. Anyone who knowingly violated any one of the attached rules would be summarily sent packing. She read further. "And do you also swear you have no known connection with any of the other contestants against whom you will be playing." Oh, dear.

Wide-eyed, she looked up at Simone and forced a smile. "I think I may have a problem." Lori felt Jason shift in his chair and she glanced at him. His mouth was firm, his expression carefully neutral, but she saw him nod and knew he understood.

"Yes, Lori?" Simone asked.

"It's this part about knowing people..." Annette's elbow connected solidly with Lori's ribs, but she went on. "You see, I already know two of the contestants, and—"

Simone stood, laid her paperwork on the chair, held up a hand to them in a signal to wait and left the room.

"Now, you've done it," Annette hissed. "We'll all be thrown out and it's your fault." She was nearly in tears.

Jason reached over and took Lori's hand. "You did the right thing, honey. You know you did." If he was lucky, Lori would be disqualified. He prayed it would come to that, even if he had to stay in the running and finish his assignment.

"And you." Annette leaned past Lori to focus on Jason. "What right did you have to encourage her?"

"I don't know what you mean."

"Oh, yes, you do. I saw you give her the signal that it was all right with you." She turned back to Lori. "Why didn't you ask me?"

Lori chewed on her lower lip. She hadn't meant to hurt Annette, but she also knew she wouldn't feel right carrying out a deception. Thank God, Jason understood that.

"I'm an awful liar," Lori told her angry friend. "You know I never could have pulled it off, anyway."

"Then you should have just told them you couldn't participate. You don't have to, you know." Fumbling in her purse, Annette found a tissue and blew her nose noisily. "Damn."

Gently kneading Lori's fingers, Jason lifted her hand to his lips and kissed the backs of her knuckles. "Do you want to withdraw?"

"Only if you do," Lori said softly.

He closed his eyes for a heartbeat and cleared his throat. "I can't."

"We could use the last days of our vacations to visit Disneyland, or the California missions, or museums—whatever you'd like."

"Lori, I can't. I'm staying in the contestant pool."

"Oh." She didn't have to pull very hard to release her hand from Jason's. He relinquished it as if he didn't care. Perhaps he didn't, she reasoned. After all, he hadn't told her how he felt about her. Why should she assume he'd given their relationship as much thought as she had? Sadly, Lori folded her hands in her lap. Annette was angry and Jason, too, was drawing away from her. She made a wry face. Some fun this game was turning out to be.

Simone reentered the room accompanied by Vicki. Lori cringed under the older woman's assessing stare.

"You know two of the other contestants?" Vicki asked.

"Yes."

"Which two?"

There was nothing Lori could do to stop what she'd started. The first pebbles had begun to roll and an avalanche must surely follow. "Annette Cole and Jason Daniels."

The look on Vicki's face was more smug than surprised, Lori decided. It was as if she'd known, already, but was pleased to hear it directly from Lori's lips.

"I see." Vicki addressed the whole group. "It was our original plan to form three-member teams and encourage you to get to know each other before the games began. I don't look forward to screening another batch of contestants and I think we can salvage this situation by putting, Lori, Annette and Jason on the same team." She raised her eyebrows. "Any objections?"

Silence reigned in the nearly empty room. Lori glanced at both Annette and Jason. Annette still had tears in her eyes, and Jason was sitting with his arms folded across his chest and a scowl on his face.

"Well, I don't mind," Lori said, "but I can't speak for these two."

"It's okay," Annette managed to squeak. "I just want to play."

"And you, Mr. Daniels?" Vicki was smiling, an expression that reminded Lori of the time her neighbor's cat had caught a sparrow and had chosen to devour it, feathers and all, on Lori's porch. Hollywood was sure a strange world.

"I have no objections," Jason said flatly.

"Good. Then it's settled. Simone will stay and answer your questions while you read the rest of the rules. I'll tell the six remaining contestants who you'll be teamed with before you leave so you can plan to get together, too, if you wish."

Simone resumed control, and Lori wondered how many thousands of hopeful contestants for other game shows had listened to the same basic discourse in the past.

"Okay," Simone said, "let's turn to the page of rules. On rule number eight, where it says, 'promise not to meet with any other contestants outside the studio,' I want you to amend it to read, 'except members of my own team,' and initial it in the margin."

Lori could sense the tension on either side of her. It seemed both Jason and Annette were upset. Well, she couldn't help that, and it *had* turned out to their advantage. After all, she and Annette knew each other better than any of the other contestants could hope to in a short span of time. They should play the game well. Providing they were speaking to each other, Lori added sadly.

She remembered that Annette had always had an unbending will to win, no matter who or what got in her way. It was hardly surprising to see it surface in a situation as charged with competition as this one was. Lori sighed. Annette was bright. She'd see the benefits of their forced alliance as soon as she was thinking rationally again.

Annette cleared her throat three times in the descending elevator before she spoke. "I'm sorry, Lori. I don't remember exactly what I said to you up there because I was so mad, but I really am sorry."

"It's okay." Lori patted her friend on the shoulder, then turned her attention to Jason. "What about you?"

"What about me? I didn't say one word against what you did."

"Well, you certainly weren't eager to withdraw, even after I offered you all of California." Not to mention my companionship, she added silently.

"I have a commitment," Jason said. "You must understand that."

"I guess I do." She took a deep breath, then leaned back against the wide, horizontal bar that encircled the wall of the elevator. "Boy, am I tired."

"And probably hungry," Jason suggested. "We weren't there long enough for a free lunch this time."

Annette came alive. "Hey! Since we're a team, let's go get a pizza. I want to get to know all about you, Jason, so we can win."

"Forever the competitor, Annette?" he asked. "Don't you ever relax?"

"Sure. Sometimes."

At street level, Jason led the way to the exit and held open the heavy glass door.

"Déjà vu," Annette said. "Are you going to kiss Lori in the parking lot again?"

Sounds good to me, Lori thought, her breath growing uneven, her pulse accelerating. Her fantasy was shattered when Jason answered, "No."

"Then I'm for ordering the biggest pizza in Hollywood," Annette told him, grabbing his hand and leading him down the street. "Come on, Lori."

Lori started trotting and finally caught up. "Nice of you both to remember me."

Jason captured her with his free arm, pulling her against his side. "You're angry."

"Me? Of course not."

"Yes, you are." He put his lips to her ear. "We need to talk."

"What about? You had the chance to spend the rest of your vacation with me and you chose *Treasure Hunters*, instead. What else is there for us to talk about?" She looked up at him. My God, he was smiling! No, he was grinning—from ear to ear. Laughing at her. Lori tried to pull away, but he held her fast.

She flashed him her most frigid look. "What's so funny?"

"You are, honey," he said. "I think you're jealous."

Walking the three blocks to an Italian restaurant, Lori had time to regain a semblance of self-control. Both Annette and Jason talked incessantly about trivialities she might have had an interest in if she hadn't been so engrossed by her private thoughts. Nothing had worked out the way she'd imagined it would. Well, she grumbled, at least Muggsy understood her.

The inside of the restaurant was dark, thank goodness, to match her mood. Lori slid into a corner booth. "I'll wait here. You go ahead."

"Get one with the works," Annette called as she and Jason headed for the counter. "I'll spring for the drinks. What'll it be, beer or cola?"

Jason's mellow laugh sent a chill up Lori's spine. "Better stay away from alcohol," he said. "You're already high on success."

"Yeah."

Lacing her fingers together, Lori watched the pair through the dimness. The restaurant had a friendly ambience that subtly lightened her mood. In a few moments Jason and Annette joined her, and Lori managed a fairly convincing smile.

She ate one large slice of the "kitchen sink" pizza, then watched in awe as Annette and Jason polished off the rest. He'd removed his coat and tie, opening the top button of his shirt, and her imagination took wing as she spied the dark hairs on his chest. If he'd been stark naked, he couldn't have affected her more. A tremor coursed through her.

He noticed immediately. "Are you all right, Lori? Can I get you something else to eat or drink?"

Can I give you a hug and kiss you senseless would be nicer, she thought. "No, thanks. I'm fine."

"You'd better be," Annette told her. "We've got to go shopping."

"Why?" Lori pushed her plate away.

"Clothes, silly. We need to find some new outfits by the day after tomorrow."

"I already have the five changes of clothes the show requires, Annette. I don't need to shop."

The bubbly blonde refused to give up. "Nonsense. We'll both play better if we feel good about our appearance." She looked to Jason for support. "Isn't that right?"

"If you say so. Lori always looks lovely to me."

Lori smiled. "Thank you. Are you all set for the show? Did you bring the proper clothing with you?"

"I suppose I could pick up one more tie and a couple of shirts. Where would you recommend I buy them?"

"I can show you," Annette volunteered. "As long as you don't go offering advice about my choices. You and Lori are both too conservative for me."

Jason saw Lori's face darken. She was upset again, or perhaps had never stopped feeling that way, and he needed to be alone with her in order to... In order to do what, Daniels? he asked himself. Are you going to make reality go away?

"Maybe Lori and I should shop together, just the two of us," he said, trying to sound calm and more in control than he felt. "I really do like a woman's touch in my wardrobe."

"What did you do in Chicago?" Lori asked, eyeing him. "You seem to have a good advisor there."

"My mother, remember? I told you about her."

Lori looked him up and down. If he was serious, his mother must have perfect fashion sense to put together a wardrobe as sensational as Jason's. For the first time, she considered the cut and fabric of his suit. It screamed "expensive" so loudly she was shocked she hadn't noticed before. Perhaps that was why both she and Annette had pictured him so well dressed. Even his casual clothes were the best money could buy.

"Tell me more about yourself, Jason," Annette said. Lori saw his posture grow visibly tense.

Before he could refuse, Annette went on, "We need to know all about you to win the upcoming game. Simone said so." She popped the last bite of pizza crust into her mouth.

Jason stood. "There's not much to tell, ladies. I'm sure you'd be bored."

"So bore me," Lori said, taking his arm. "We want to win."

"Okay. While we shop for my new tie. But we can't all fit in my car." He'd spent the past hour trying to decide how to get out of showing Lori the Ferrari and stirring up more questions. "Where shall I meet you?"

"Glendale Galleria," Annette said. "Do you know where that is?"

"I'll find it."

"Okay, meet us on the first level by Marni's Intimate Apparel. I need to buy a shorter slip."

Lori snorted derisively. "I didn't know they *made* slips as short as you like them."

"Smart aleck." She went over the directions with Jason, then turned to Lori. "Of course, you could ride with him, if you were willing to let me drive the Mustang."

"Over my dead body," Lori said. "I loaned it to you once and you scratched it."

Jason opened the restaurant door and held it for them. "Badly?"

"Well," Annette hedged.

"It was bad," Lori answered. "Where are you parked? We can caravan so you don't make any wrong turns." And I can keep my eye on you, she added. In her wild imaginings about Jason, she'd even entertained thoughts of following him home to see what he was hiding.

"I'm afraid my car is several blocks in this direction," he lied. With a wave, he backed away. "I'll see you there."

As he walked up the street, Lori turned to her friend. "Why did you ask him to meet us by that particular store? He's bound to be embarrassed."

Annette giggled. "I know. I just love to see him blush, don't you?"

"When did you see him doing that?"

"He does it all the time."

Lori was losing patience. "When?"

"When he sneaks a peek at you and you're not looking. I saw him do it at least three times during lunch."

Lori took her by the arm. "Come on."

"Where are we going in such a hurry?" Annette had trouble making her shorter legs keep up with Lori's determined strides.

"To head him off at the pass," she answered. "I don't want to be late getting to the mall and take the chance he'll think he's missed us and leave." She also intended to circle around the block and try to spot him in traffic. Not that she thought she'd succeed, but it was better than doing nothing.

"Have you been watching too many late-night Westerns or has being in Hollywood gone to your head? You're starting to talk a little crazy."

"Crazy, yes," Lori agreed. "But it's not Hollywood that's driving me there, believe me." She looked over her shoulder. Jason had disappeared from sight.

Chapter Seven

For Jason, the drive to the mall was enlightening. It gave him the time he needed to pull his thoughts together. He knew that the more he saw Lori and her friend and the more he relaxed, the more likely he was to commit an error that would lead to his unmasking.

He couldn't chance it. Not with so much at stake. Hell, if he failed this undercover assignment he could probably kiss his hard-won career goodbye.

Driving like a madman, he cut across two lanes of traffic to the Glendale freeway. His teeth were clenched. Whatever happened with regard to his job, he made up his mind he'd learn to live with the consequences, just as long as he didn't have to kiss Lori Kendall goodbye.

Shocked at his train of thought, Jason hit the off ramp at thirty miles an hour over the speed limit, gripped the Ferrari's wheel and whipped into a parking space in the Galleria lot.

He sat motionless. He'd just considered throwing away his entire life's work for a few blissful days with Lori.

Breathing unevenly, he climbed out of the car. If he trashed his career for her, what would he have to offer her in a week's time when his assignment was completed?

Jason crammed his keys into his pocket and started for the mall at a run, ignoring the stares of shoppers. At this point, he had little choice; play it smart or risk losing a financially secure future. He had to think rationally for both their sakes.

Forcing himself to move more slowly, Jason entered the state-of-the-art mall. The afternoon crowds were so thick he was afraid he'd be nearly on top of Lori and Annette before he spotted them. That wouldn't do. In order to have the advantage, he had to remain unseen.

He started to walk toward a glass elevator that rose through a jungle of tropical plants. It wasn't a perfect escape route, but it would have to do. The faster he reached the upper levels, the safer he would be.

The elevator door slid closed and the glass cylinder began to rise. Jason stared blankly at the wall and mentally went over his plan. He'd locate Lori from above, phone the lingerie store with an excuse that he'd been detained, then watch to make sure she got his message.

The elevator came to a smooth halt. Jason stepped out, located a map of the mall and a pay telephone and placed himself at the second-story railing to wait.

"I *told* you he wouldn't like this store," Lori said.

"Phooey. He's a tourist. He just got lost or something."

"Lost, my eye. I've ridden with him. He has an uncanny sense of direction. I don't think you could lose him if you tried."

Annette pulled a face. "Well, I didn't try, if that's what you mean."

A soft voice spoke from inside the store. "Excuse me. Is one of you ladies Lori Kendall?"

"I am." Lori cocked her head to one side. "Why?"

"There's a message for you," the clerk said. "Mr. Daniels was supposed to meet you here, but phoned to say he couldn't make it."

"Thank you." Lori's heart was pounding so hard she could count the beats in her temples by simply holding her breath. She found she'd been doing just that and let it out with a whoosh.

Annette was still pouting. "It's not my fault."

"Of course it isn't," Lori said. "Come on. We're here, so we might as well get some shopping done." She pushed open the door and entered the small shop.

"What do you think happened?"

"I don't know." Lori lifted a sheer blue nightgown, wondered immediately if Jason would like it on her and dropped it as if it were the hot end of her curling iron. "He'd borrowed a car from a friend," she said. "Maybe it broke down."

"Yeah. That's probably it. Well, forget him. Let's spend till the plastic in our charge cards melts."

"Sure." It wasn't likely she'd forget Jason Daniels, not today, not ever, Lori thought sadly. She succeeded in producing a wan substitute for a smile. I hope he's all right, she fretted, unable to quiet the uneasy stirrings coursing through her.

The hair on the back of her neck prickled and she froze, looking out through the wide windows that stretched across the front of the store. Funny, she thought, I feel as though I'm being watched.

Annette called to her. "Ooh! Come see what I found."

With a shrug, Lori turned away.

For Jason, watching her go was a lot like watching the sun disappear behind a cloud. It would be a day and a half before he'd see Lori again. An eternity. Yet he didn't dare even telephone. The way he was feeling he was liable to open up and confess everything. And ruin both their futures, he thought with chagrin.

Jason walked slowly down the mall, took the next available escalator and made his way back to his car. The big question, now, was what to do with himself for the next thirty-six hours.

One special place came to mind. One place that harbored happy memories of holding Lori in his arms and listening to her intoxicating laughter.

Climbing into his car, Jason headed for the beach at Santa Monica.

True to her word, Simone was waiting to welcome them under the awning in front of Affiliated Broadcasting. Her broad smile was pleasant, but did little to alleviate Lori's jitters. Lori lugged her folding garment bag to the porch and dropped it. "Oof. That's heavy."

Not far behind, Annette groaned. "Yours is heavy? What about me? I'm four inches shorter than you are."

"But you wear less clothes," Lori quipped.

"Very funny." Letting her bag sag to the ground, she joined the group crowded around Simone. "Hi, everybody!"

Dead silence greeted her.

"Oops." Annette grinned sheepishly at Simone. "I forgot."

"It's okay to be friendly when I'm here to supervise you," Simone told them all. "The no-talking rule only applies to the times when your baby-sitter—namely me—is not around."

Giggling, Annette asked, "You're going to the rest room with us, too, I suppose?"

"I sure am." Simone laughed at her shocked expression. "It takes a little getting used to, but believe me, we have our reasons."

The roar of a powerful engine caught Lori's attention. She looked in the direction of the sound, as did everyone else in the group. A sleek red sports car entered the parking lot, screeched around a line of cars into the nearest aisle and came to an abrupt halt next to her Mustang. Behind her, Lori heard one of the men whistle and comment on the cost of such a toy. The driver, dressed in a long-sleeved shirt, dark tie and beige slacks, climbed out.

Lori turned to Annette. "Why doesn't that surprise me?"

"It does me!" Annette gasped. "Geez-louise. I guess his excuse for standing us up at the mall wasn't car trouble."

Lori nodded, pressing her lips together. "I guess not."

"Sorry if I'm late," Jason said, joining Simone and the others.

"I'll let you come in as late as you like if you'll take me for a ride in that car," Simone teased.

Lori saw a funny look erase Jason's earlier smile.

"Tell me you don't mean that," he said.

"Of course I don't," Simone said quickly. "I always joke around. It makes everybody relax."

Looking from Simone to Jason, Lori wondered what had happened to Simone's good humor. And to Jason's. A pall settled over the group of contestants. All business, Simone had them gather up their clothing and follow her.

Passing through office corridors and out again into the sunlight, Lori noticed that Annette was hanging back. "Hurry up."

"This darned garment bag is too heavy."

Simone had paused at the entrance to a large, hangarlike building. "Everybody *together*, please."

"We're coming." Lori was about to pick up the lower end of Annette's bag when the weight of her own was lifted.

"I'll take them," Jason said.

Lori squared her shoulders. "That won't be necessary."

"Nevertheless, I want to help and we're holding up the rest of the contestants." He took Annette's burden as well. "Follow me."

Annette laid her hand on Lori's arm. "What's the matter with you? We're supposed to be a team, remember?"

"I remember. I also remember that he promised he'd phone and he didn't."

"Don't be silly. Sure he did. You just weren't home."

"I wasn't?"

Checking her manicure as they walked, Annette said, "No. You certainly didn't stay home every second waiting for him to call, did you?"

She had. Like a fool. "Of course not."

"Well, then, you see? Give him a break."

They passed down the center of a wide corridor strewn with scenery panels, lights and assorted technical apparatus. "It looks like a junkyard," Lori marveled. "And why is it so cold in here?"

A willowy girl with short brown hair spoke up. "That's to keep the television cameras happy. They don't work well in the heat."

"Oh." Lori's eyes widened. Along one wall was a glass case at least twenty feet long, filled with signed photographs of celebrities. Through an open door she could see a maze of brightly colored scenery and hear an audience applauding. "This is amazing."

The girl smiled. "Haven't been in a TV studio before, have you?"

"No. Does it show?"

"Yes. But you'll be an old hand by the time you're done. This is my second try at fame and fortune." She laughed. "Well, at least fortune. I'm an actress. They don't let you say that on the air, so I have to settle for winning grocery money till I'm discovered."

Lori walked closer to her and pointed at Jason's back as he preceded them down the hall. "What do you think of him?"

"Luscious. Why?"

"No, no. I mean, is he like most of the contestants you've known?"

"Oh, because of the Ferrari?" She arched one perfectly sculpted eyebrow. "Didn't you say the other day that you already knew him?"

"A little."

"People do this kind of thing for other reasons besides money, you know. Maybe he's on an ego trip."

"Maybe." Lori followed the group into a mirror-lined room. The floor was made of worn hardwood and there was a dancers' exercise bar along one wall.

Simone clapped her hands for attention. "Name tags are on the table. Find your place, pin on the tag and sit in that exact chair. I'll need to see your driver's licenses and social security cards to double-check your identities."

Lori slowly walked the length of the table. The folding chairs were arranged in groups of three. Her name tag was placed between Jason's and Annette's. A momentary flutter turned her empty stomach upside down and she wished she'd forced down some breakfast in spite of the fact that her first bite of toast had given her the hiccups.

Beside her, Lori felt a strong presence. Jason's hand lightly caressed the middle of her back.

"I'm glad you wore that peasant blouse and blue skirt again," he said. "You look very pretty." He helped her sit down. "Did you go shopping with Annette?"

"I went. I didn't buy much." She looked over at him as he joined her. "Where were you?"

"I telephoned the store."

"We got your message. That still doesn't tell me why you suddenly decided not to meet us."

"I couldn't."

"You couldn't? That's all?" She folded her hands in her lap, clenching them tight. "I thought we were friends."

His hand drifted from the back of her chair to her shoulder. "We were. We *are*." Leaning closer, he brushed his cheek against hers and whispered, "Please, Lori. Trust me?"

"I want to. I really do, but—"

"Then that's all I ask for now. Here comes Vicki. We'll talk later."

The knowing look Vicki gave the group made Lori wish she was back in the days of Mrs. Fensterwald. She sighed. Oh, well. She was here. Jason was here. And whatever his reasons had been for deserting her at the mall, he certainly seemed penitent enough now.

You don't own him, Lori reminded herself. He may have kissed you and made you forget every other man you've ever known, but he made no commitment. She snorted cynically. No *commitment*? He hadn't even seen fit to tell her where he was staying while he was in California!

Wise up, Lori, she told herself. If he cared for you he wouldn't have so many deep, dark secrets. He wouldn't need them. He'd trust you.

Forcing herself to concentrate, she listened to the drone of Vicki's voice. Too bad I don't really have a mind like a detective, Lori thought. If I did, I'd know what's wrong with this whole situation.

"Any questions?" Vicki asked, jarring Lori back into the real world. "Good. Then we'll proceed to the studio and get acquainted with the stage." She started to get up, then waved her hands for everyone to stay. "Wait, wait. I almost forgot. You need to hear the speech about not cheating from our illustrious Fair Practices Department."

A young girl whose presence Lori had overlooked came to the front of the room. She was slightly built and looked barely twenty-one.

"My name is Ruby," she said. "I'm here to make sure this game is conducted fairly." She hoisted herself up onto the top of an empty table and sat with her legs dangling over the edge. "Because if you so much as look like you're cheating, you'll be booted out of here so fast you won't know what hit you."

"Sweet," Annette whispered.

Lori shushed her with a finger to her lips.

Smiling, Ruby launched into a series of rules and regulations. As she read the last one, she added, "The easiest way to make sure no one trips you up is to do only what you're told and speak only to me, Simone, Vicki, or each other. Anytime you're in doubt, don't."

"This is *jail*," Annette whispered. "And I thought it would be fun."

Jason leaned around Lori to speak to Annette. "It will be fun. You'll see. You'll forget about how closely you're being watched, loosen up and have a ball."

He grinned like a little boy at Ruby when he saw her stare. "No problem here. Just explaining."

"Then maybe you'd like to explain how the questions are chosen?"

"No, no. You go right ahead."

Ruby got down from her perch, picked up a clipboard and pencil and stood quietly. "I'll be the one who makes the final selection. Since I'm not associated with the production company, there can never be a challenge to the honesty of the draw. Are there any questions?" She waited. "No? Then that's all. Good luck."

Bright girl, Jason thought. Stay calm and stick to the regular sequence so you don't leave anything out. He'd have to remember to put a commendation for Ruby in his report to McAlister.

Simone was standing by the door, clapping her hands. "Line up over here. You don't need your bags. We'll lock the room so everything will be just as you left it when you get back."

Falling into the ragged line, Lori stepped up beside Jason. "How is it you're such a pro?"

"I've been in this situation before," he said blandly.

"Did you win?" Lori's curiosity about him was driving her up the wall. She hadn't had any luck asking about his job or home life. Maybe a less personal question would fare better.

"Win?"

"Money? Prizes? You know." What an exasperating man!

"I got a fair amount of money for what I did, yes."

"Was it out here in Hollywood? What show were you on?"

Jason shook his head. "No. It was back home in Chicago. A little station that only broadcasts locally."

He hadn't exactly lied to her, Jason told himself. She hadn't asked him if he'd been a contestant; only if he'd received money for his efforts. He figured wages counted as well as winnings.

Simone led them down the hall and stopped by an alcove. "This is your last chance to use the bathrooms before we go into the studio," she said. "As soon as Ruby checks to make sure no Affiliated Broadcasting staff members are using them, you're free to go in." She chuckled. "I strongly recommend it. You'll be nervous on stage."

"She meant it!" Annette said loudly, eliciting giggles from most of the group. "Geez-louise, I haven't been escorted to the bathroom since I was five years old!"

Ruby gave the all clear and Lori dragged her friend into the ladies' room. "Be quiet and do as you're told. This was your idea, you know."

"Yeah, but I wasn't expecting this. I don't know if I can stand much more of this kind of treatment."

"You want to win, don't you?"

"That's a dumb question."

"Then pull yourself together and stop complaining. Remember the prizes and the money."

Annette did a parody of her favorite announcer. "Some of our departing contestants will receive..."

"That's the spirit. Think like a winner and you'll be one," Lori told her. "Now, fix your lipstick and let's get back to Simone before she sends bloodhounds after us."

Giggling, Annette pursed her lips and colored them a bright red once again. "We could cut across the swamp, dodge the alligators and escape into the forest."

Lori took her by the shoulders and forced her out the swinging door into the hall. "March!"

The stage was smaller than Lori had expected it to be. From the way quiz shows filled her television screen she'd assumed the sets had to be massive. As it was, the backdrop with its flashing colored lights and geometric patterns was probably no more than thirty feet across. Dozens of enormous lights hung from metal tracks below the vaulted ceiling.

Each of the three sections of the stage was done in a contrasting color scheme. On the left of the set was the blue area, in the middle was the yellow section and the red was on the right.

Banks of empty seats faced the stage. Lori climbed the steep aisle ahead of Jason and slid sideways into a row marked Contestants.

Tucking her skirt under her, she settled herself into the narrow, padded seat and smiled at him. "Cozy, isn't it?"

He sat down, laying his arm over the back of her chair. "I kind of like it." His fingers found the bare part of her upper arm and he began to stroke her gently.

Lori took a deep breath. "You said you wanted to talk to me?"

"Later."

She nodded slowly. "Always later. Why is it, every time I'm with you, I feel like a Senate investigating committee quizzing an underworld figure about his back taxes?"

Jason laughed quietly. "You have a wonderful imagination, honey. We're going to have a lot of fun together." For the rest of our lives, if I have anything to say about it, Jason told himself. His hand tightened on the arm he was caressing.

Lori knew from experience that he'd gone off on one of his mysterious mood swings again. His expression was so solemn, his body so tense, she wanted to lay her hand on his brow, smooth away the frown and kiss him till she exorcised whatever demon was hounding him.

Sensing her concern, Jason smiled at her. It had been months since he'd broken off with Monica and he wanted to make love to Lori so badly he hurt all over. The muscles in his jaw knotted. When he thought of how close he'd come to settling for marriage with Monica when Lori Kendall was about to burst into his life like fireworks on the Fourth of July, it terrified him.

Lori laid her head on Jason's shoulder. It felt good to be near him. More than good, it felt right. The only thing missing was his trust. Having it was crucial, but how she could gain it, she had no idea.

Vicki stepped onto the raised platform in the center section of the stage. "Annette, Jason and Lori will be called the red team. Val, Jean and Larry will be the blue. And the remaining three will be the yellow team. Can I see the red and blue teams down here first, please?"

Obediently Lori and the other five chosen contestants lined up under the bright stage lights. Jason held her hand all the way.

"I'm nervous," she said.

He gave her fingers a reassuring squeeze. "You'll do fine. This is just the walk through. It's like a dress rehearsal. Don't worry."

Vicki was joined by a man with dark, wavy hair, clad in a jogging suit. Lori knew from looking at him that he'd never worn that particular outfit for exercise. Nor was he likely to, she added, judging from its expensive cut and the lack of stretching room in the right places.

"This is Brian O'Connell, our master of ceremonies," Vicki said.

Dutifully Brian shook hands with each contestant. "So, are you all ready to work your way to the treasure?"

Too enthusiastic, Lori thought. He seemed nice enough but awfully insincere. And the way he kept rubbing his hands together reminded her of a surgeon getting ready to operate.

"Good! Then let's get started." Brian peered at Lori's name tag. "Lori! Into the isolation booth!"

She allowed herself to be led off camera by a man wearing a headset and sporting enough wires for him to be officially classified as a robot.

He placed her at the edge of the carpeted platform. "Stay here."

"Wait," Lori called. "Where's the isolation booth?"

Brian ignored her. "Now, Annette and Jason, I'll ask you each to give me a quick response to a word, and Lori will have to guess which of you the chosen word comes from." He looked at Jason. "The word is 'state'!"

"Illinois," Jason said.

"And you, Annette?"

A grin split her face. "California!"

"All right, let's bring Lori back onstage now," Brian called loudly.

With a flourish, he welcomed her. "Lori, the word was 'state.' One of your teammates gave the response, 'Illinois.' Was it Jason or Annette?"

"But, I was standing right there and I heard—"

Brian shushed her. "We know that," he said quietly. "This is so the directors, the sound and lighting people and the cameramen can get their equipment properly adjusted. It also gives you some practice. Just play along, okay?"

It was a relief to hear Brian O'Connell speak without shouting every sentence. "I think it was Jason!" Lori said, clapping her hands in delight.

"Right!" With a sweep of his arm, Brian indicated seven flashing numbers on a board behind them. "And that answer entitles you to a choice of clues to the hidden treasure. What number do you want?"

"Six?"

"Number six. Let's put clue number six up on the red team's side of our scoreboard while I go and meet the blue team."

Lori felt Jason's hand take hers again and she looked up into his eyes. "This is like living on an alien planet."

"In a way. When we have the remote microphones on, we won't be able to talk to each other privately, either."

She raised her eyebrows. "Thanks for the warning."

"You're welcome."

Annette drew them both into a huddle. "Speaking of privacy, I know how we can win this part of the game, for sure. But we've got to get together where no one can overhear." She thought a moment. "Lori's place. We'll meet there tonight after dinner. Okay?"

Watching his expression, Lori didn't doubt that Jason was struggling to come to a decision.

"We could follow *you* home and meet there," she suggested innocently. "That is, if you have some objection to coming to my house."

"No, no. I was just thinking about something else," he said. "Your place is fine. As a matter of fact, why don't I follow you home?"

Annette giggled. "Gee, Mom, it followed me home. Can I keep it?" She dodged Lori's playful punch, her fancy footwork carrying her to the edge of the stage. A stern look from Vicki sent her scurrying back to Lori and Jason. "Oops. You said I'd forget myself and have fun, but I think I just overdid it."

"Probably," they both said. The accidental unison of their reply struck them both as funny.

"My parents used to do that all the time," Lori said. "It always amazed me."

"It's wavelengths," Jason said. "I believe some people are naturally attuned to each other."

"That's impossible."

"Is it?" He placed one finger under her chin to raise her gaze to his. "What about the first time you and I met?"

Lori's breathing grew labored. "I was surprised by the elevator door. That's all."

"Were you? I didn't see it quite that way."

Here we stand, Lori thought, in front of dozens of strangers, and now Jason decides to get romantic.

Swallowing to moisten her dry throat and not succeeding, she smiled sweetly. "You don't seem to see anything the way I do, Jason."

"For instance?"

Lori had hoped for a more private confrontation, yet she didn't want to pass up such a perfect opportunity to be frank with him. "Honesty and openness, for instance. Where I come from, people who like each other don't keep secrets."

"I'll bet they do," he countered, letting his hand slip to her shoulder where his fingers teased her exposed skin.

A disembodied voice boomed through the studio. "That's good, Brian. Now I'd like to get some volume levels on the contestants."

Startled, Lori jumped away from Jason.

He grinned at her. "Don't worry, honey. That's just the director. He sits above us in a glassed-in booth where he can see everything that happens."

Annette clasped her hands to her chest. "Wow. I thought the place was haunted." Giggling, she pointed at Lori's surprised face. "You look like you're as nervous as I am."

"Why shouldn't I be?" Lori asked, leading her aside. "All you've got to think about is the show. I've got Jason Daniels, too."

Peeking around Lori, Annette winked at him. "It does seem so." She whispered behind her hand, "Aren't you glad I invited him to your place tonight?"

"I would be if I thought he really wanted to come. I got the feeling he'd rather not."

"Nonsense. He's probably shy."

Stepping aside, Lori pointed at Jason. "Look." A male audio technician had clipped a tiny microphone to Jason's tie and was in the process of threading a wire under his shirt and connecting it to a transmitter the size of a small transistor radio.

Lori could see part of Jason's midsection as he lifted his shirt. He was totally unperturbed about being partially undressed in front of the crew and the hundreds of spectators now filing through the doors and filling all the empty seats in the audience.

"Do you see that?" Lori asked, pointing to Jason's bare skin and trying not to blush noticeably.

"So? Nice muscles, but so what?"

"Does that man look shy?"

Annette blushed. "Nope."

"I rest my case."

Secluded behind a privacy screen to the right of the stage, Lori waited as a female audio technician clipped a microphone to the eyelet trim on her blouse and Ruby stood guard nearby. The sending unit fit easily inside the waistband of Lori's skirt.

The audio tech then turned to Annette, baffled as to where to stash her sound system.

"There's no extra room inside this dress," Annette protested. "You can't stick it down there."

"We can usually hang it on a woman's bra if all else fails," the tech said. "But there's no back on your dress."

"There's no bra, either," Lori told her. "How about letting my friend hold the box for now?"

The woman shrugged her shoulders. "Guess I'll have to."

Ruby escorted Lori and Annette back to Jason. In the time Lori had been away from him she'd thought of lots of other things she wanted to say. Unfortunately anything she told him from now on would be instantly broadcast.

"Is everything okay?" Jason asked.

"Peachy." Antagonism born of frustration crept into Lori's voice. When Jason put out his hand to touch her, she moved aside.

"Annette?" His plea for the other woman's intercession was genuine.

She tossed her frizzy hair. "Don't worry about her, Jason. She's just bent 'cause you won't tell her where you hang out. She'll get over it. She's really crazy about you."

"Annette!"

The loud voice filled the studio once again, and Lori swore she could see the lights in the rafters quiver. "Tell your contestants to keep their minds on the game, will you, Vicki? It sounds like the plot for an afternoon soap opera from up here."

One icy stare from Vicki was all it took to quell Annette's tendency to babble. Lori felt sorry for her friend. This was her big moment, the one she'd cried and sweated for, yet if she didn't exercise more self-control she was likely to either lose or be replaced before the game started.

Lori had been so busy with her own problems, she hadn't noticed Brian O'Connell was missing until he reappeared in a suit and tie. He stood under the lights while one person combed his hair and another dusted powder on his nose.

Stage managers placed Lori's group shoulder to shoulder, then did the same for the opposing team.

When the man wielding the powder puff patted Lori's nose, she looked up at Jason. "Are we still practicing?"

The director's voice boomed. "Hasn't anybody told the contestants this is for real? Let's go, people."

"Real? Geez-louise!" Annette's knees started to buckle and Jason caught her with an arm around her waist.

"It's a game, Annette. A *game*. That's all it is. Remember that."

She sagged against him for a second, then breathed raggedly and squared her shoulders. "Gotcha. A game. Ooh, boy!"

Lori knew Jason was only being helpful by assisting Annette, but did he have to touch her? She laughed inwardly at her jealous reaction. Oh, she had it bad all right if a simple gesture of friendship was enough to tie her stomach in knots and play havoc with her imagination. You're supposed to wish the best for your friends, Lori reminded herself, not turn green if they happen to garner the attention of a mutual acquaintance. She tried to put aside the rivalry she felt. In the back of her mind a little voice echoed, "But did he have to touch her?"

Offstage, beyond the brightness that limited her field of vision, Lori heard someone counting, "Three, two..." A woman wearing a headset stepped into the circle of light, just beyond the view of the cameras and finished her sentence. "One." She pointed her index finger at Brian O'Connell, and Lori saw him come alive.

"Good day, ladies and gentleman. Welcome to *Treasure Hunters*, the game show that leaves the studio and travels all over the land. Maybe we'll be in your area soon and you'll have a chance to cheer our contestants to victory! Let's meet them, shall we? On the red team we have Lori, Jason and Annette. Let's start with Lori. Tell us about yourself!"

The words tumbled out of her mouth in what she felt must have been a fairly intelligible sequence. Lori saw Brian smile, nod and move on, but if anyone had offered her a million dollars to repeat her introduction, she couldn't have done it. Nor could she have told anyone anything about what the rest of the contestants said. It was as if she were a sleepwalker: there in body, absent in consciousness. Part of

her wanted to be alert and participate, while another part
wanted to run off the stage. The end result of her internal
conflict was a near catatonic state.

Lori felt Jason's arm around her waist and leaned toward him. That way, if she collapsed, he could let her down
slowly, she reasoned. In the dimmest recesses of her mind,
she heard bits of conversation.

"And, now, Lori, one of our helpers will put you in our
isolation booth."

That was Brian's voice, Lori told herself. She smiled. Nice
man, Brian. Always happy. Not like Jason. Her vision
wasn't the clearest, but she knew some men in pirate cos-
tumes were guiding her steps.

"This one's a zombie," one of them said. "What'll we
do?"

"Put her in the booth and keep smiling," the other answered.

Lori sat down as the door closed. Someone pressed a glass
of water into her hand. "Drink this."

"Mrs. Fensterwald?" Lori took the plastic cup and
sipped the contents. Slowly she began to focus her thoughts.
"Oh, Vicki. Thanks."

"Get a grip on yourself. You play the game well. Just
think about what I taught you, not about where you are,
and you'll be fine."

"Yes, ma'am." Lori's self-awareness was returning in
waves. "What happened to me?"

Vicki reclaimed the cup. "Don't worry about that. You
looked and sounded perfectly normal. I knew you were in
trouble and I suppose your team members did, too, but the
audience didn't notice anything."

Shaking her head, Lori stared at Vicky. "I honestly don't
remember."

"That's okay. You can watch your performance on TV in
a month or so and relive the whole thing." She paused, her

brow furrowed. "That is, if we get picked up for the fall season."

There was a knock on the booth door. "Okay. You're on," Vicki said. "Remember to breathe, Lori, and try to keep your concentration focused on the game, not on the cameras."

"I will." Escorted to the edge of the platform, Lori felt a push from behind and she rocketed onto the set. Jason looked worried and Annette—poor thing—looked as if she'd just heard she'd won the state lottery and couldn't find her winning ticket.

Brian greeted her. "Lori! Here's the original word, drawn from our drum by a member of your team. When I said 'stubborn,' which of your teammates answered with 'man'?"

"Oh, dear. I don't know."

"You have six seconds, Lori," Brian warned.

Milliseconds before a buzzer sounded, Lori blurted out, "Annette!"

"Yes!" Applause filled the room. "You may now choose a numbered clue to the treasure and that clue will be yours in the final round of *Treasure Hunters*."

"Number six," Lori said, surprised at how poised she felt. This game-show stuff wasn't so hard. All you had to do was think on your feet, keep breathing so you didn't fall flat on your face and not throw up on camera no matter how jumbled your insides were. A piece of cake. Her thoughts made her smile.

Instantly Jason touched her hand. "That's better," he whispered, his free hand cupping the tiny black mike clipped to his tie. "You had me worried."

"I'm fine." Lori placed her own hand lightly over her microphone. "It gets easier as you go along."

His face glowed with emotion. "So does love."

Lori stood there with her mouth open, realized what she was doing and resolutely closed it. "What did you say?"

"Later," Jason said. "It's our turn to play again."

Chapter Eight

Lori sighed, leaning back in the folding chair and staring at her weary image in the mirrors behind the ballet bar. "One thing about *Treasure Hunters*. They may work us into a stupor, but they sure feed us well for the effort."

"The condemned ate a hearty lunch, dinner and bedtime snack, right?" Annette looked at her watch. "Can you believe it? It's eight-thirty!"

Jason stood behind his two team members and leaned on the backs of their chairs. "I'm sorry. I didn't think to warn you. Taping sessions like this can run all day and into the evening if the producer's on a tight schedule."

"I only got to wear two of my outfits," Annette wailed.

"There's always tomorrow," Lori told her. "We're due back here at 10:00 a.m."

"If I live that long."

Jason pulled back both their chairs, paying special attention to Lori. "I suppose you're too tired for the get-together Annette wanted."

She started to agree, then changed her mind. Jason owed her an explanation of his earlier reference to love, among other things. Maybe if he was tired enough he'd inadvertently reveal some of the things she wanted to know.

"Not at all," Lori said. "Let's plan to caravan, as you suggested."

"Oh."

His expression was so forlorn, she couldn't help pitying him. The more time they spent together, the more she cared for him. Conversely the more she also feared what he might eventually tell her about himself.

Lori looked into his eyes. Either she was overtired and imagining things, or there was genuine pain showing in his expression. When he took her arm she voiced no objection. Just as she had needed to lean on him when she was suffering from stage fright, so he now seemed to covet her strength for his own sake. It was good to feel she was a necessary part of his life.

"I can't stay long," Jason said.

Lori nodded and slung her purse over her shoulder. Her team had gone through one change of wardrobe in order to tape a second day's show and she was wearing the turquoise silk dress with tiny pearl buttons that Annette had insisted she bring. Not that seeing her in the flowing, seductive dress had apparently affected Jason Daniels, she mused. So much for Annette's ideas about attracting a man.

Walking beside her, it was all Jason could do to retain a semblance of his self-control. Lori's full-skirted dress covered her amply, yet it was still the sexiest outfit he'd ever seen. Correction, Jason told himself. Lori Kendall was sexy. The dress was merely the shimmering dust on the butterfly's wings. The butterfly he didn't dare capture. Not yet. Not without risking the death of what they might someday have together.

Simone escorted the group to the outside door and bid them all good-night.

"Are you sure you want me to come?" Jason asked.

"Yes, of course. Besides, you owe me an explanation, mister. I may have been stunned by the lights and cameras, but I distinctly recall the word 'love' being bandied about."

"I'll follow you," Jason said quietly. He placed their bags on the back seat of Lori's car and walked to the Ferrari.

Before Lori's coffeepot had finished brewing, Annette was sleeping soundly on the living-room couch.

Jason followed Lori into the kitchen, accepted a cup of the steaming brew and seated himself at the small oak table in the corner. He rolled up his shirtsleeves and removed his tie, draping it over the back of the chair. "I shouldn't even be here," he said.

She slid one of the ladder-back chairs closer to his side of the table, purposely making their conversation intimate. "Neither should I."

His laughter was cynical. "You live here, Lori."

"You know what I mean." She stared, unseeing, into the steam swirling up from her cup. "I shouldn't be with you."

"You don't mean that."

"Yes, I do." Looking past him she went on, "I've been playing mind games with myself for too long." Her eyes misted and she blinked back tears.

"Lori, please..." Jason reached for her hand, his expression solemn. "I didn't use the word 'love' by mistake. You must know that." As his fingers captured hers, he felt her tremble. Damn, Jason thought, this situation shouldn't be so difficult. In two more days—three at the outside—he'd be able to tell her everything. Why couldn't she be more patient?

"I know that love is more than a wonderful feeling, Jason. At least it is to me."

"It is to me, too, honey." He knew with one short sentence of confession he could win her trust. And then what, Daniels? he asked himself. The answer came easily. Telling her would put Lori in the same untenable position he was trapped in, only it would be much worse for her. He, at least, had entered his profession willingly. Lori would have to lie to her best friend and become a consummate actress overnight to protect his job. Or, she'd have to choose to violate *his* trust, instead.

No. He couldn't ask her to make a choice like that. If he loved her, which he certainly did, then he'd have to prove it by continuing to protect her from what would happen if he told her the truth. That was all there was to it. End of argument.

"I want to believe you, Jason. I want to with all my heart." Lori lifted her free hand and caressed his cheek, trailing a tender path down his jawline.

He grasped her wrist, brought her palm to his lips and kissed it. "Oh, honey. Please give me a little more time."

"We only have a few days. How can you expect me to surrender to my feelings for you when I'm the one doing all the giving?"

Jason slid his chair away from the table and drew her into his lap, cradling her against his body. "You're not the only one, Lori. Believe me. And I wasn't just trying to lead you on by saying I love you."

When she raised her head to look at him, her lips were soft, pliant and moistly inviting. Casting aside all his reservations about involvement, Jason brought his mouth down on hers. Lori trembled, then met him on his terms. He kissed her again. Hard. He'd suffered and needed and denied himself for too long. This was the woman he was going to marry, whether she was ready to admit it or not, and he wanted to possess her.

Placing her hands on Jason's shoulders, Lori tried to push him away. Her resistance was a feeble attempt at retaining her sanity and she knew it. Truth to tell, she wanted everything he was offering her—and more. In her heart of hearts she loved him unequivocally. It was insane. It was hopeless. But it was true.

Breathing raggedly, Jason pressed her closer and felt her nails dig into his shoulders. His tongue parted her lips and found a welcome he'd only dreamed of. He moaned softly, the sound rising from his innermost being.

Lori's arms wound around his neck, her fingers sweeping through his hair and tantalizing the back of his neck. She wanted Jason Daniels as she'd never wanted anyone before. One of his hands played across her ribs and rose to cup her breast, lighting a fire within her she knew could never be extinguished.

"Oh, Jason, I know it's crazy, but I do love you."

"Lori." Opening the top button of her dress, Jason slipped his fingers beneath the silk. "I need you so much."

"I know." She pulled his head down, met his kiss with equal fervor and slid her tongue across his lower lip before plunging it deep into his mouth.

The result was as she'd hoped. Jason lost the last of his restraint. His hands roamed restlessly over her breasts, back and hips. She shivered as he pushed aside her skirt to caress her thigh. His touch was warm, demanding and oh so exquisite.

"Tell me to stop, Lori," he whispered, "or there'll be no turning back."

She shook her head. "I don't want to make any decisions. Don't you know that? I don't want to think or be sensible. Not tonight."

"Oh, Lori."

She had just settled her head against Jason's chest when the silence was shattered.

"There you are!" Annette was rubbing her eyes as she staggered into the kitchen. "Why'd you let me go to sleep like that? I told you I wanted to plan our strategy." She made her way to the sink and poured herself a cup of coffee.

Lori placed two fingers lovingly over Jason's lips. She knew it would be hours before she recovered, physically, from his kisses. Emotionally—well, references to eternity kept popping into her head. Breathing hard, she straightened her dress and returned to her own chair.

Loathe to let her go, Jason grasped both her hands in his and mouthed the words, "I love you."

Lori echoed his sentiment and added aloud, "I swear, I'd forgotten she was there."

Jason's laugh was little more than an exercise in self-mockery. "I know. So had I."

Seemingly oblivious to the disastrous timing of her entrance, Annette joined them at the table. "You see, the answer came to me while we were playing today. All we have to do is decide to give one set of say, five words, that will fit into the context of the game and we'll eliminate all the guesswork."

She sipped her coffee. "It's like this. We pick one color for each of us, red for me, blue for Lori and green for Jason. And one emotional word, like love or something. Then we each plan to do one state, like we did in practice and so on. No matter what Brian asks us, we always give one of our preselected answers. See? It's brilliant!"

Lori's mind was not on Annette's harebrained schemes. She still pictured herself in Jason's arms, feeling so wanted and so a part of his life that it didn't matter what tomorrow brought. The last thing she wanted to think about was the game show.

"Uh-huh," Lori said absently. A sense of abandonment coursed through her when Jason abruptly released her hands and rocked back in his chair.

He focused all his attention on Annette. "Go on."

"That's about it. It'll work. I know it will. If we stick to my plan, we can't lose."

Scowling, he leaned his elbows on the table and laced his fingers together. "I think you're right."

"I know I am." Annette poked Lori with one manicured nail. "And so do you."

Lori merely shook her head and sighed. "I guess so." The wonderful part of the evening was obviously over, she told herself with deep regret. Looking at Jason, she found no remaining sign of his ardor. He seemed to have readily forgotten how close they had come to making love.

She cringed inside. In retrospect she could see it would have been a big mistake to surrender to Jason in the heat of the moment. Logically she'd always known that.

A tear formed in the corner of her eye and she brushed it away. As much as she knew it would have been foolish to have given herself to him, she still wished, secretly, that he'd carried her off to bed.

"I've got to be going," Jason said, rising and taking his cup to the sink.

"Hey, would you mind giving me a lift? I only live a few blocks from here." Annette smiled and yawned. "That way, Lori won't have to do it."

Jason nodded. "Sure. You go on out. I'll be there in a minute to load your bag into my car."

"Great. Thanks."

Alone once again with Jason, Lori didn't know what to say. He was walking slowly toward her, but his hands were stuffed in his pockets. A man who was about to deliver hugs and kisses didn't act like that, Lori decided with chagrin.

"I'll see you in the morning, honey."

"Yes, I suppose you will."

"It was better this way."

Agreeing, she lowered her lashes and averted her gaze, embarrassed by the memory of her wanton behavior. "Don't worry," she said. "I know that one night does not a future make."

"But one night can destroy a future," Jason told her tenderly. "Someday you'll understand."

She lifted her eyes to his. "Will I?"

The distrust he saw in her face made Jason's heart ache for her. Would there be enough days in his entire life to love away that hurt? Dear God, he hoped so.

"Give me three more days, Lori. Just three more days."

"Do I have a choice?" She folded her arms.

"No, I guess you don't."

Shrugging, she nodded. "Good night, then."

Lori stood alone in the silence for a long time after she heard the Ferrari drive away. One possible explanation after another occurred to her and she rejected each in turn. Finally she walked slowly back to the kitchen.

Clutching a mug of coffee, she sat at the table and stared at the wall. It didn't matter what Jason was hiding from her. Not really. The only thing that *did* matter was his lack of trust. He'd sworn he loved her and maybe in his own confusing way, he did. The trouble was, no matter how they felt about each other, their relationship was impossible. Lori sighed. It had been doomed from the start. The only mistake she'd made was in forgetting that fact.

It was 3:00 a.m. before Jason finished his detailed report to McAlister. Out of professional courtesy, he ran off an extra copy for Halpern-Oldham before shutting down his computer. *Treasure Hunters* wouldn't work, at least not in its current format, and Jason felt he owed it to everyone involved to expose the flaws before any more money was invested.

He rose and paced across his ultramodern living room with its vaulted ceilings, white-and-chrome furniture and unobstructed view of the ocean. What good was all his monetary gain if he had no one to share it with? Jason asked himself.

Thoughts of Lori haunted him. The look in her eyes when she'd bid him good-night was one of utter disappointment. Would she think any better of him when he was able to tell her the truth?

Standing at the bay window, he faced the moonlit Pacific. He'd have to handle his revelations to Lori very carefully, making sure she understood the scope of his job and his reasons for hiding it from her.

Maybe a candlelit dinner in some out-of-the-way place, some champagne and soft music? That was good, he decided. And a ring? Jason shook his head. No. Lori was the kind of woman who'd like to choose her own engagement ring.

Pleasurable feelings filled him. With the proper planning and careful execution, the wooing and winning of Lori Kendall would be the most enjoyable task he'd ever undertaken.

Jason smiled to himself. They'd share a glass of champagne; then he'd take her hand, tell her what he'd been doing as a contestant on *Treasure Hunters* and ask her to marry him. So easy. The perfect culmination to a stormy, whirlwind affair.

He closed the drapes and climbed the spiral staircase to his bedroom, picturing Lori's responses to his proposal. She'd smile, he decided, taking off his shirt. Then she'd throw her arms around him and smother him with passionate kisses. Grinning broadly, Jason headed for the bathroom and a cold shower.

"I'm beginning to think of this place as home," Annette said.

Lori leaned out the car window to give their names to the gate guard, then pulled into the Affiliated Broadcasting lot. "It's more like summer camp," she said. "Everybody's really friendly, yet you know you'll never see them again, once this is all over."

"Except for me and Jason."

"Except for *you*." Lori parked and got out. "I don't think I'll be seeing Mr. Daniels."

"Oh, come on, Lori. You know better. He's crazy about you."

"He's also going home soon. What do you expect me to do, follow him to Chicago?"

"You could ask him to move out here." Annette laid her garment bag on the fender of the Mustang while she waited for Lori.

"People who care about each other don't try to manipulate each other's lives, Annette. If Jason wanted to move to California, he'd have said so."

"Unless he's waiting for you to ask him."

"Phooey. You don't know the half of it." She put her bag over her shoulder, grasping the hangers in one hand and her purse in the other.

"I'm willing to listen if you think it will help."

"You're a good friend," Lori told her, "but I really don't want to discuss it." She sniffled. "It's liable to make my mascara run if I do."

"Heaven forbid! Your eyes would get puffy, and I left my cucumber slices at home!"

"Okay, okay." Lori laughed at Annette's melodramatic outburst. "I'm smiling." She displayed a forced grin. "See?"

"That's better." They were almost to the awning. "What do you think our chances are? Honestly."

"It matters a lot to you, doesn't it?"

"Like life and death." Annette stopped walking. "Before we go in, have you memorized the list of words I gave you?"

"Annette, I . . ." Lori knew it was futile to argue with her friend. She'd tried to tell her that morning that she thought it was wrong to decide on prearranged responses. Annette had refused to listen to reason.

Sighing, Lori nodded. She knew what words Annette had chosen for each team member. Most of them would probably have been Lori's natural choices, anyway. If, in the course of the game, those same words came to her, then she'd say them just as she would have before Annette's meddling. If they didn't... Well, Annette would have to understand.

"Look, there's Jason," Annette said. She handed her bag to Lori. "Hold this while I give him his list."

"Annette. You shouldn't." Lori searched for the argument that would deter her friend before she got herself in big trouble. "What if you're seen?"

"Not a written list, silly. I'll whisper it to him."

Lori watched Jason's face. He seemed uninterested to the point of rudeness, barely acknowledging Annette's presence. As soon as she left him he glanced briefly at Lori, then turned and joined the other contestants on the porch.

"Did he agree to do it?" Lori couldn't believe he would. Of course, there had been a time when she wouldn't have believed it of Annette, either, she thought solemnly.

Annette pouted. "No. All he said was we didn't need special words today. We're moving on to the rebus puzzles." She pressed her lips into a thin line. "Drat."

Lori sighed with relief. Now she wouldn't have to choose between her friends and a compromise of her principles.

Squaring her shoulders, she adjusted her pale pink, fringed scarf so the knot was fashionably off center and smoothed the flowered print of her sundress. The bright, Hawaiian print was more casual than her other outfits. She'd chosen to wear it, not for glamour, but to lift her spirits.

Goodness knows, my spirits need lifting, Lori thought seriously. If her friends at the aerobics studio had told her a week ago that she'd be hopelessly entangled in both a television production *and* a star-crossed love affair, she'd have laughed in their faces.

"You're fine, Lori," she muttered to herself. "Just fine. Nothing happened that can't be rectified by the passage of time. Several aeons should do it."

Her subconscious disagreed, inexorably drawing her gaze to Jason's broad back. Philosophical arguments were useless where he was concerned. She saw him look over his shoulder at her and felt her strength and resolve ebb like the tide. He didn't even have to smile to turn her inside out.

Quickening her pace, she forced herself to look away and join the group.

The first puzzle was "Custer's last stand." The blue team solved it in twelve seconds, making Annette so nervous she was nearly in tears.

"Now, red team, are you ready?" Brian O'Connell asked, shuffling the three-by-five cards in his hands.

Lori cast a sidelong glance at Jason's imperturbable profile. Annette's hands were clasped so tightly together that her knuckles were white and her eyes were as wide as a frightened rabbit's. Lori shook her head. One member of her team didn't seem to care if they won or lost, while the other was so jittery she was probably equally useless. Well, Lori mused, at least *she* had her wits about her.

"Good!" Brian shouted. "We'll see how well you do right after a word from our sponsors." He grinned affably until the all-clear sign from the stage manager. "If we had any sponsors," he deadpanned.

The woman with the headset smiled at him. "Don't worry, Brian. You can always go back to summer stock and do Shakespeare."

"And starve?" he countered. "I'd rather be wealthy than literary, thank you."

"Wouldn't we all?" She clamped one hand to her ear, listening. "Okay, people. Counting." Stepping back, she held up her fingers, "Five, four, three, two, one," and pointed.

Brian's whole persona changed. "Well, here we are with Lori, Jason and Annette, going for their sixth clue. Are you ready?"

"Yes!" Annette blurted out. "Let's go!"

Surprised by her friend's sudden burst of enthusiasm, Lori looked at her questioningly. Somehow, Annette had managed to dredge up a sizeable dose of confidence while she'd been preoccupied with watching Brian O'Connell. Now, if only Jason could generate an equally impressive change of disposition, they'd be in good shape to win.

She glanced at him. If anything, he seemed more detached than he had before. The clues were coming up on the storyboard, one per second, and Lori had no more time to speculate on his moodiness. She forced herself to forget the strange attitudes of her teammates and concentrate on the puzzle.

Lori had already figured out several of the syllables when Annette screeched, "Remember the Alamo!"

"Right!" Brian pointed to their list of numbers. "You have only the numbers one and seven left to choose from. As soon as one of our teams gets all seven clues on their side of the board, we'll move on to the third level!"

"Number one," Annette said, watching the lighted numeral appear behind her.

"And that means the red and blue teams are tied, ladies and gentlemen." His smile never faltered. "Let's have our next puzzle while I go over to Jean, Val and Larry on the blue team."

"Hold it." The director's voice echoed through the studio. "I want to tape that last sequence again. We had some problems."

Lori saw Ruby motion Brian off the set and hand him a new stack of answer cards. "What happened?" Lori whispered.

"I don't know," Annette insisted. "Why ask me?"

Lori turned to her other team member. "Jason?"

"She knows, all right," he said.

"I do not."

Her frustration at a peak, Lori covered her microphone. "Will somebody please tell me what's going on?"

"She cheated," Jason said. "Got a look at Brian's cards and saw to it that we won."

"Annette wouldn't do that."

"She not only would, she did." He cocked his head to one side. "Why do you think Ruby picked new questions?"

Lori stared from Jason to Annette and back again. He certainly seemed positive about his allegations. She supposed Annette's flash of intuitive brilliance could have been misinterpreted as cheating.

"Please, you two," Lori said. "Let's remember we're a team."

"Yeah, Jason," Annette parroted. "We're a team."

"You don't have to remind me."

Lori was getting disgusted with them. "You sound like brother and sister, fighting over who was supposed to do the dishes." She was watching Brian out of the corner of her eye. "Now behave yourselves before I disown both of you."

Lori greeted Brian with a gracious smile as the taping resumed. With the way he held his cards in the palm of his hand, she didn't see how anyone could have glimpsed the answers.

Seconds ticked away. By the time their current puzzle was entirely revealed, Lori was certain it must be in a foreign language. Neither she, nor Annette nor Jason knew the answer.

"All right, red team," Brian said, drawing out the agony. "Your time's up. If the blue team can solve your puzzle in less than ten seconds, they'll have their seventh number and *Treasure Hunters* will move on to its last and most exciting phase!" He wheeled away, leaving Lori alone with her already grumpy teammates.

"I still don't have an inkling," Lori whispered, frowning at the letters and pictures that made up the rebus. "I think it's 'Mary . . . something,' but that's as far as I get."

Annette grabbed her arm. "For heaven's sake, be quiet!"

No noise came from the audience, the cameras rolled into position on silent rubber wheels and Lori held her breath. Just a few more seconds and her team would gain another chance to accumulate clues, she thought. Just a few more...

"Mary, Mary quite contrary!" the blue team shouted. A loud bell clanged. Larry, Jean and Val jumped and hugged each other while Annette bit her lower lip.

"Right!" Brian gestured toward the blue team's number board. Only the five was missing. "We'll give you your last number and I'll explain the rest of the game to you and our audience."

He smiled and faced the nearest camera. "Each clue is in a sealed envelope, to be opened by our teams when they reach the treasure site. They'll be given ten minutes to figure out the clue, get to the area described and rescue the colored *Treasure Hunters* flag. Our grand prize will go to the team that gathers the greater number of flags!"

Brian turned to Lori's group. "You have only five of the seven possible clues, red team, but don't give up. If you solve your clues quickly and beat the blue team to four out of the seven sites, you'll be our big winners! And remember, contestants, each flag is also worth one thousand dollars!"

Saluting the camera, Brian said, "Be sure to tune in tomorrow and watch our players go the last mile! See you then," and he waved goodbye.

Lori took a deep breath. "We can win if we pull together." She scowled at Annette's expression of defeat. "But not if you think we're already beaten."

"I know it. I can't help how I feel. Nobody can."

Boy, isn't that the truth, Lori mused. She'd managed to keep from flinging herself into Jason's arms, but the desire was stronger than ever. She chuckled to herself. It was a darned good thing for her that he was acting so aloof. One of his warm, genuine smiles would probably turn her to mush, and then who would hold the red team together in its final minutes of glory or defeat?

Simone and Vicki approached, rounding up Lori and the other contestants like sheep. Audio technicians stripped the microphones from them as they walked, disconnecting the thin, black wires and unceremoniously pulling them out from under each contestant's clothing. As usual, everyone was in a hurry, Lori noted, wondering if she was going to manage to get any rest at all on her soon-to-be-ended vacation.

Lori and the other women were separated from the men and hustled into a windowless area decorated like a waiting room. On the settee were plastic bags containing red, yellow and blue lightweight sweat suits in varying sizes.

"These are your team colors," Vicki said. "Find the size you need and get it on; then choose a new pair of tennis shoes from the row over by the door." She waited. "Well? Get moving. You have ten minutes to be dressed and ready to go. We're taping day four this afternoon."

Annette grabbed Lori by the hand. "Come on. Head for the smallest ones and help me. You know I'm too short for regular sizes."

Chuckling, Lori let herself be dragged across the room. "What do you expect me to do, alter it to fit you in ten minutes?"

"Maybe we could pin it? I brought safety pins."

"And maybe you'll wear it as it comes," Lori said. "At least try one on before you panic."

Val and Jean were pulling on their blue sweatpants, laughing and stumbling over each other. Lori reached out to steady Jean, then went back to Annette.

"It'll never work," Annette wailed. "Look!" The pants alone reached her armpits and she was standing on the bottoms of the legs.

Lori didn't know what to say. She tried to maintain a bland expression, but couldn't. She nodded. Her lips twitched and she broke into uproarious laughter.

The other women in the room joined in the fun. "You don't really need a top," Jean said. "You're well covered like that."

"The newest in sweat suits," Lori added. "Strapless!"

Annette tried to mope, but the high humor was contagious. "I haven't been this covered up since I played an Egyptian mummy in my high-school play."

The tall girl who'd told Lori she was an actress postured in her yellow outfit. "Look at me, ladies. The only job I'll get from appearing like this, is a stand-in for an underripe banana!"

Lori slipped her sweatshirt over her head and shook her head to free her hair. "I do like the pirate's treasure-chest logo on the front, though. Kind of makes me feel rich, already."

"Yeah." Annette hiked the pants up as high as she could, then carefully lowered a shirt over them. "Gold and silver always were my favorite colors."

"I like green," Jean said, "as in money."

Lori grinned. "There are more important things in life, you know." She exploded into laughter again when everyone else in the room asked, "What?"

"Okay, okay," Lori said. "I give up."

Annette was hanging upside down off the edge of the couch, fluffing her wildly disarranged hair. "Don't mind my friend, ladies. She's not rational. She's in love."

"Annette!"

"I wish I had a dollar for every time you've yelled my name like that." She straightened, took out her makeup bag, and put blusher on her cheeks.

Jean smiled maternally at Lori. "He seems like a very nice man."

"Who?" Lori looked at herself in the mirror. Thanks to the turn of the conversation, her cheeks were so flushed she couldn't tell if she needed more makeup or not.

"Your teammate," Jean said. "That was who your friend meant, wasn't it?"

Lori sighed. "It was. Only I'm afraid things aren't going to work out for us."

Zipping up her case, Annette made a face at Lori in the mirror. "Right now, you couldn't give me that man if a million-dollar check went along with him—tax free. But that doesn't mean he's not the one for you."

"He's not."

"Phooey." Annette hiked up her sweatpants. "Anyway, I don't have time to argue the point with you. Let's get our shoes on before Vicki makes us go back onstage barefoot."

Tying the stiff, new laces of a pair of red tennis shoes, Lori wondered what Jason was thinking of while he dressed. As much as she chose to deny it, her fondest hope was that his mind was filled with sweet memories of her.

Chapter Nine

Bathroom time," Simone called. "Remember what your mamas used to tell you and be prepared. We're going for a little ride in the country."

Lori followed Annette into the ladies' room. "I'm beginning to identify with Alice in Wonderland. Every time we turn around, reality shifts and we're involved in something else. This TV business is bizarre."

"But profitable," Annette said. "Keep seeing the dollar signs."

"I never was in it for the money, and you know it. Truthfully I'm not sure how I let myself get tangled up in this scheme of yours." Lori leaned closer to the mirror and touched up her lipstick, then led the way back to Simone.

The whole group was escorted to the parking lot where they were unceremoniously loaded into vans. The vehicles departed, forming a caravan that entered scenic Griffith Park a few minutes later.

Lori gazed out the window at the steep, brush-covered hillsides of the popular park. Bridle paths marked by white rail fences paralleled the road, crossing it occasionally.

Warm breezes ruffled Lori's hair. The pleasant aura of early summer bathed her in tranquillity, lifting, for the moment, the burden of her concerns about Jason.

Three vans, color coded to each *Treasure Hunters* team, climbed the winding road. Following closely was a much larger vehicle containing Brian O'Connell, mobile cameramen, technicians, the man with Muggsy's eyes, Vicki and Simone and assorted support staff.

The red team was privileged to have Ruby along for security, while other, equally serious-looking individuals from the Fair Practices Department accompanied the other teams.

Lori chose to sit next to the van's driver, leaving the rear seats for the others. It wasn't that she didn't want to sit by Jason, she told herself, it was simply a matter of self-preservation. Her every waking moment was already filled with thoughts of him. If she wasn't careful, there would be no room in her life for anyone or anything else. She couldn't take a chance on that happening. Not if she expected to resume a normal existence after he was gone. Lori laughed at herself. Who was she trying to kid? It was already too late to recapture the person she'd been. Jason had seen to that.

The red van pulled to a stop in an outlying portion of a parking lot. In the distance the triple-domed Griffith Observatory was outlined majestically against the clear blue sky.

"It's a good thing it's not hot today," Annette grumbled. "I'm already roasting in this darned suit."

Lori pivoted in the bucket seat and swung her legs over the left side to look back at her friend. "That's because you're wearing two layers. If they let us take these outfits home, I'll shorten those pants for you tonight."

"Thanks." She slid open the side door of the van and jumped down, carefully sizing up her surroundings as Ruby herded them all toward the other vehicles.

"I'll bet the observatory figures in this somehow," Annette whispered to Lori.

"You could be right. I wonder who has our clues."

Jason stepped closer. "I imagine that Ruby does. That's her job." He let Lori and Annette move on ahead of him. Lori couldn't be involved in a plan to cheat, no matter what Annette had tried to make him believe, he argued. Not Lori. She was too honest.

But are you letting your personal feelings for her alter your opinion in her favor? Jason shook his head thoughtfully. Damned if he knew anymore. In the case of Lori Kendall, he had long ago ceased thinking and behaving like a professional.

He closed the gap between himself and his teammates in time to hear Annette say, "I wish we didn't have to drag *him* along."

From that distance Jason couldn't hear Lori's soft-spoken reply, but he did see her nod her head affirmatively and had to presume she agreed. The assumption hurt all the way to the secret recesses of his heart. Unintentionally he resurrected the protective wall around his feelings that he'd abandoned soon after he'd met her.

Lori's skin began to tingle, her throat tighten. Without a doubt, Jason was watching her. She glanced back in time to see his expression harden. Although it was obvious he was angry, she had no idea why. Given the circumstances, it seemed to her that Annette was the one who had every right to be upset, not him.

Flashing him a slight smile in spite of his conspicuous displeasure, Lori was rewarded with a noncommittal tilt of his head. Men, she thought cynically. They were all unfathomable, and Jason Daniels was the worst of the lot.

She tried to convince herself she'd be happier when he was out of her life and had gone back to whatever it was that he was unwilling to divulge. Probably something nefarious like taking candy from babies or purposely singing off-key in the church choir. For the sake of her slipping sanity, she tried to imagine Jason involved in more heinous crimes. It was no use. To her, he was marvelous. Stubborn, sensitive, mysterious, unique and just plain wonderful.

Thoughtfully she considered his taciturn expression, the almost sinister look he'd given her. There was a lot to be said for the masculine way of expressing hostility, Lori thought. Besides being easier on the eyes, a stiffly unbending stance gave the man the edge in any kind of combat, be it verbal or physical. And it sure beat grabbing for a Kleenex every time you got mad.

"Are you ready to play?" Jason asked.

Startled out of her daydreaming, Lori jumped while her stomach did a backward dive and landed in her toes. "No. But I guess it's too late to back out now." Having long ago set aside thoughts of why she had been brought to Griffith Park, she meant it was too late to go back and avoid becoming romantically entangled with Jason. The statement seemed clear enough to her, given her recent musings.

Annette misunderstood. "Back out? Geez-louise, Lori, you've got to be kidding!"

"That's not what I meant," Lori said, laying a comforting hand on her friend's shoulder. "Don't panic. They couldn't carry on with the show if we quit."

Jason's voice sent jolts of electricity singing up her spine. "Sure they could. Why do you think the yellow team is here?"

Lori shrugged her shoulders. "To watch?"

"To be ready to step in. This is just a pilot. Remember? They need a complete show from the first contest to the final treasure hunt. Who plays is of a lot less importance."

Annette bristled. "That's nonsense. Don't listen to him, Lori. He's just mad because we aren't ahead. We'll show him. We'll show everybody."

Rolling her hazel eyes toward the heavens, Lori took a calming breath. "I feel like a delegate at the UN peace talks," she finally said. "Will you two please try to get along?"

"I have no problem with that." Jason extended his hand. "Annette?"

Begrudgingly she shook it. "Okay. Truce. Only you'd better help us win, mister, or there'll be war for sure."

"Agreed."

Lori sighed. "Oh, good. An armed truce. Welcome to an instant replay of the siege of Vicksburg. Which one of you wants to represent the Confederacy?"

She saw Vicki motioning to them. "Never mind. Come on, troops. Our general awaits."

Brian O'Connell was the picture of suave sophistication mixed with a liberal dose of intrepid daredevil as he faced the contestants. "All right, red and blue teams. You've selected your first clues. They're in sealed envelopes. Are you ready?" Holding a microphone in one hand, he brought his other hand down with a broad sweep of his arm. "Go!"

Annette's overly long nails made it difficult for her to tear open their envelope. Shaking with excitement, Lori tried to help her and dropped it. Caught by the afternoon breeze, it fluttered away.

Jason retrieved it and dusted his footprint off the outside. "May I?"

"Yes, yes," Lori said. "Open it. Hurry!"

He unfolded the paper, stared for a moment, then began to smile. "It's a limerick." He started for their van. "Come on."

Lori almost collided with a cameraman in her haste to peek over Jason's shoulder. "What does it say? Where are we going?"

"If I read it aloud, the blue team may overhear and eventually figure it out. They chose clue number one. That's why I suggested we start with the highest number we had and work backward."

"Makes sense to me," Annette commented. "Grab the map of the park Vicki gave us and let's get moving." She gestured to one of the men with a mobile camera rig resting on his shoulder. "Follow us!"

Jason slid open the van's side door and spread the map on the seat. "Both of you study this while I read the clue."

"Gotcha." Breathless, Lori wasn't sure how much of her rapidly deteriorating physical condition was due to a new case of stage fright and how much was due to the commandingly exciting figure Jason became when he asserted himself as their leader.

He read,

"There once was an engine so fine,
Which came to the end of the line.
It gave up one day,
And here it must stay.
Our flag is but one of the nine."

Jason put down the clue and bent over the map. "Engine? Where would we find an engine?"

"Here?" Lori pointed. "It says Traveltown. There's a scale-model railroad that runs all the way around it."

"No," Jason said. "This one's parked. The poem says it came to the end of the line. It can't be operational."

"Get in the van!" Annette squealed. "That has to be the place!" She hauled the hapless cameraman in behind her. "They said we have to take you so you can film us finding the flag, but they didn't say we had to let you slow us down."

"What about Ruby?" Lori asked, forgetting she didn't want to sit next to Jason and moving to the back of the van. "Doesn't she have to come?"

"You bet she does or I'm out of a job," the van's driver replied. "And don't any of you get ideas about speeding, either. I have orders to stay within the posted limits."

"Everybody remember to smile," the cameraman said. "Vicki's monitoring from the mobile unit." He perched the minicam on his shoulder and took his place in the front as Ruby joined them.

Annette was bouncing on the seat. "Come on! Roll!"

Ruby nodded to the driver, laid her clipboard on her lap and they were off.

Scarcely a quarter of a mile had passed before Jason moved near Lori. "Hi."

"Hi, yourself." She busied herself studying the passing scenery.

"I think we may finish this up by tomorrow."

"Does that please you?" Keeping her face turned away from him was the only way she could control her turbulent emotions and keep from asking him why he was angry and why they seemed to be drifting farther apart as the day wore on. His nearness was almost too much to bear. It tugged at her heart, at her body, until she was trembling inside. She clasped her hands tightly in her lap.

"Of course. Aren't you excited to see who wins, too?"

"Yes." She paused. "I just hope it's Annette, for her sake. This whole experience means so much to her."

"I know," Jason said quietly. "Some people should never place themselves in situations so charged with energy. The competitive urge can get the better of them and they wind up doing things they wouldn't dream of under normal circumstances."

Lori's head snapped around. "You mean like cheat?"

"Yes."

"I don't believe you, Jason Daniels. You're determined to smear Annette's name, aren't you?" She shook her head. "You'd rather assume she sneaked a look at the answer than admit she's simply a good player."

"She is a good player, or she wouldn't have gotten this far, Lori." When he reached for her hand she pulled away, so he crossed his arms. "Okay. Have it your way. But I still maintain that your friend cheated." Jason's voice grew low and husky. "And I think you know it."

"You what?"

"You heard me."

"I certainly did." Unfastening her seat belt, Lori got up, leaving Jason alone in the back of the van.

Annette was studying the map when Lori joined her. "What were you and Jason doing back there all nice and cozy? Planning your next date?"

"I have a great idea," Lori said, fighting tears. "Why don't you be quiet and give me a Kleenex?"

Annette folded the map and tucked it into the pocket in her sweat suit. Concern was evident in her expression. "Hey, I'm really sorry. As usual, I wasn't thinking. I know this whole game-show business has been rough on you and you're only here because of me. I want you to know I do appreciate what you've done."

"That's okay." Lori sniffled. "I'm sorry I was rude to you just now, too."

"Hey, what good are friends if we can't dump on each other once in a while, huh?" Annette smiled broadly. "But you'd better knock off the gloomy look. We're on TV, remember?"

Her predicament was so ironic, it struck Lori as morbidly funny. "I can hear the newscaster now. 'Television game-show contestant breaks all precedents by crying *before* losing! Film at eleven.'"

Annette playfully punched Lori's shoulder. "Who said anything about losing? We're gonna win, you hear? I'll see to it single-handedly if I have to."

What an indomitable spirit, Lori thought. What an unbeatable attitude. Jason was so wrong about Annette. He must be judging her by standards he acquired in his unsettled childhood instead of seeing that her strong will and belief in herself was what had made her a winner.

A man like that was not what she was looking for to plan a secure, stable life with, Lori admitted sadly. The chemistry between them might be extraordinary, but it took more than a few stray pheromones to make a long-lasting partnership.

Will you please stop avoiding the word marriage? she lectured herself.

It doesn't matter what you call it, her subconscious countered, it's what you want.

No, I don't.

Yes, you *do*. The realization hit her squarely between the eyes. For a long time she'd kidded herself into believing she was happier alone and independent, answering to no one. The advent of Jason Daniels in her life had changed all that, almost overnight.

Deep within her the fires of love for him smoldered, growing ever larger, ever more powerful, no matter how hard she tried to extinguish them. And now what? she asked her heart. Why did you let me fall in love with him?

Some things are inevitable, her heart answered. Some things were meant to be and nothing can change them.

Traveltown was nestled in a valley of the park, a green oasis amid brush-covered hills.

"Pull up right by the gate, driver," Annette ordered. "We want to be close."

"I have to get out first, lady, to film you," the cameraman said. "Let me stand over by the gate. Okay?"

"Okay, but hurry it up." Annette slid open the door. "Scoot!"

Laying her hand on her friend's arm, Lori smiled at her. "I think we'll do better if you calm down. The poor man's just doing his job."

From behind her she heard Jason say, "For once, you and I agree on something." He got out next, extending his hand to Lori and Annette. Neither took it so he nodded and stepped aside. "Where shall we begin?"

"At the train," Annette said. "The engine."

Uncomfortable with the seriousness of her recent revelations about love in general and Jason Daniels in particular, Lori was unusually quiet.

Muttering to herself, Annette was gazing at the colorful displays and leading the way across the narrow-gauge tracks into Traveltown.

"You'd better look where you're going," Lori warned. "Here comes the train." An attendant slid a white picket-fence-style gate across the tracks, effectively isolating Annette from the rest of her party.

"Hey! You can't do that. We have to stay together!" Annette focused her attention on her teammates. "Don't just stand there." When no one moved, she added, "Jason, do something!"

"What?"

"I don't know. Something?" Annette was frantic. "Ruby? Help?"

Lori also looked to Jason for a solution. "What can we do? We're losing precious time."

"Cross the tracks," he said. "Give me a minute." Jason vaulted the fence and approached the guard. They spoke quietly together, then Jason jumped back across to his companions. "He says he'll look the other way if we hurry."

Jason lifted Ruby by the waist and easily swung her into his arms. "Sorry about this. I know we haven't been properly introduced. Is there anything in the rules that says I can't throw you around in the interest of fairness?''

Giggling, she clutched her clipboard to her chest. "I don't think so.''

"Good." Jason put her down beside Annette. "Wait here.''

His second trip was for Lori. Rather than be carried, she chose to jump the fence unaided.

"Hey," Jason accused, "I'm supposed to get to rescue you.''

"You're forgetting my profession," Lori countered. "I'm capable of getting over fences by myself.''

"Do you leap tall buildings in a single bound, too?''

She shot him a disgruntled look. "If I had a good enough reason, I might.''

Jason laughed. "I believe you would." He offered his hand to the cameraman.

"They didn't tell me this would be hazardous duty," the man quipped.

"Me, either," Jason said. "This job is full of surprises, isn't it?'' He clamped his jaw closed. The questioning look on the cameraman's face could be dismissed without explanation, but if Lori had overheard his slip of the tongue he might be in deep trouble. So, what else is new? he asked himself. She already thinks you're on a witch-hunt, with her best friend as the innocent victim.

Helping the cameraman scale the opposite fence, Jason rejoined his team. Annette was walking away, and he fell into step beside Lori. If she'd heard his conversation, she gave no outward sign of it. One thing was for sure, though, he owed her an apology for insinuating she was purposely protecting Annette. He'd blurted out the ridiculous accusation in the wake of his anger and frustration. Lori deserved kinder treatment.

"I'm sorry," he said softly.

"For what?" Her head was tilted back, her eyes scanning the buildings for the elusive flag.

"For doubting you." I slipped back into my profession, where I was supposed to be all along, he thought wryly, and it immediately got me in trouble. "I should have known you'd never tolerate cheating."

Lori almost smiled, then managed to look duly stern. "Yes, you should."

"Am I forgiven?"

His voice caused what was left of her sensitive nerve endings to vibrate. She gave him her most endearing grin. "Yes. I'm sorry, too."

"You are? Why?"

"Because I was blaming you for something you can't help." Lori slid her arm through his, savoring his natural strength through the fabric of his sweatshirt.

Every muscle in Jason's body tensed. She *couldn't* know the truth. It was impossible. Yet it sounded as if she'd figured out his whole deception and was issuing a blanket pardon!

Turning, Jason grasped her shoulders. "Go on."

She lifted her face to look into his compelling eyes, oblivious to the whirring television camera. "There's not much more to say, Jason. We're all products of our pasts. You see things differently than I do. You always will. Neither of us can change what we are."

She paused to gently stroke his face, smoothing away the frown on his forehead with loving fingertips. "I know it's not your fault you have to go back to Chicago any more than it's your fault I fell for you like a lovesick child. It just happened."

His breath escaped with a whoosh. "Oh, honey. I don't know what to say."

"Then shut up and kiss me," Lori ordered. "We've wasted enough time playing silly games."

Jason hesitated until he saw the cameraman pan to the right to follow Annette's progress. What the kiss lacked in duration it more than made up for in intensity. Jason's conscience hammered at him while he channeled his frustration into that one brief expression of his love.

Lori stepped back. "Wow! Do the ladies in Chicago know you can kiss like that?"

With a throaty laugh, Jason pulled her to him. "Hell, *I* didn't know I could kiss like that till I met you."

She eased back in his arms, her palms pressing against his thudding chest. "Jason, please. Let's just have fun and not get serious."

"I'll try." The smile he gave her enveloped her like welcome summer sunlight on a garden of blooming wildflowers. "But I won't guarantee I'll succeed."

Placing her hand in his, Lori started after Annette and the rest of their entourage. "Neither will I."

"Is that so bad?" Jason's fingers had intertwined with hers.

She could only shake her head. Tears were threatening again, tears of happiness and loss combined. "It's not fair, you know," she finally said.

Jason slipped his arm around her waist. "What's not?"

"The way I feel."

His hold tightened. "Tell me."

"It's complicated. I don't understand it completely, either, but it reminds me of the way I felt when my older sister hid my favorite teddy bear." Again his warmly affectionate laugh bathed her in love.

Lori pulled a face. "I bare my innermost secrets and you laugh."

"I'm sorry, honey. I was just picturing myself as your teddy bear and it struck me funny." He struggled to keep the smile off his face. "Tell me, did he sleep with you?"

"Every night," she said, blushing. "He was my best friend, too."

"Then I do like the idea of applying for his job," Jason said. "Is there an opening, or did your sister finally return him?"

"She returned him." They had almost caught up with Annette. "I'd carried him around so much his seams kept coming undone. My mother mended him and so did my grandmother. You could always tell where I'd been playing by the trail of teddy-bear stuffing."

"So, you retired him to a drawer?"

"No." Lori was shocked that the memory was affecting her so deeply. "One day I found a beautiful, new, pink teddy bear on my bed. The old one was gone without a trace."

Jason gathered her into his arms. "Now that I do understand." He planted a light kiss on the top of her head. "I'll bet you searched for him for a long time."

"Years, actually. I told you I don't give up easily when I set my mind to a puzzle. Which reminds me..." Lori glanced over Jason's shoulder, her eyes focusing on a distant building housing antique fire trucks. Fire engines.

"Jason! Look!" Pointing and gesturing, Lori screamed, "That's it! Nine flags!"

He grabbed her hand. "Well, come on! Annette! Ruby! Follow us."

Dodging tourists who stared at them as if they were either demented or worse, an example of typical Californians, Lori and Jason dashed across the reproduction of a town square to the fire station. Above the door was an arch and atop that, fastened directly in the center, was a flag bearing the same logo they wore on their shirts.

Annette skidded to a stop. "That's it! We've found it!" Glancing rapidly from side to side, she sobered. "How'll we get it down?"

"We need a ladder," Lori volunteered. "Did anybody bring one?"

"Very funny," Annette said.

Jason stepped into the building, returning a moment later with a red-painted, wooden ladder. "You two steady it for me and I'll get the flag."

"Be careful," Lori warned. "This ladder isn't the greatest."

"Oh, shush and let the man climb. To listen to you, a person would think you cared about the guy."

"No more than my teddy bear," Lori mumbled to herself.

Jason stretched, strained, then straightened, waving the captured flag over his head. The gathering crowd below cheered. He saw an older woman wearing a camera around her neck approach Lori.

"What is all this for, my dear? It looks like lots of fun."

Lori opened her mouth to answer as Jason yelled from the top of the ladder, "Lori! No! If you talk to her you can be disqualified."

She snapped her mouth shut, replying to the woman's question with an apologetic shrug and a lift of her eyebrows.

Jason was beside her in seconds. "That was close."

"Yes. Thanks for the warning." Wordlessly she helped him return the ladder to the attendant waiting just inside the door. "But there's something I don't understand."

"What?" Jason guided her back to the group.

"How can it be against the rules to talk to other people when we've all talked to the cameraman and our driver? They're not on our team, either."

"I know. It is confusing. Theoretically, as a contestant, you're supposed to hold conversations only in Ruby's presence and not speak to anyone not specifically okayed ahead of time."

"Will that work in public places like this? It seems to me too many people would forget."

He nodded agreement. "I think you're right. This whole game has a lot of problems in its organization."

"Well, where to, now?" Lori asked as they rejoined the others. "Can we get our next clue here?"

"No," Ruby told her. "We have to go back to the central location. Brian will present you with your second envelope in exchange for the flag." She beamed at Jason. "Congratulations."

"Thank you."

Annette fell into step beside Lori while Jason tried gracefully to extricate himself from a conversation with the Fair Practices representative.

"You can see that Ruby likes Jason, too," Annette said. "Too bad we can't get him to cozy up to her a little and—" The look on Lori's face was stern enough to shut off Annette's stream of chatter.

"You don't mean that, do you?"

"Of course not. I was only having some fun with you."

"Well, don't kid about stuff like that," Lori warned. "Some people, who shall remain nameless, are already sure you cheat."

"You told him that was ridiculous, didn't you?"

Lori studied her friend's face. "If I thought for one minute that he was right, I'd quit the game."

"Oh, don't be silly." Leaving Lori behind, Annette trotted after the cameraman. "Wait! I want to ask you some questions about that fascinating camera."

"She never gives up, does she?" Jason asked, catching up to Lori.

"You'd have to know her as I do to realize she's behaving normally."

He took her hand. "And how about you, Lori? Are you?"

"Normal?" Heavens, no. I haven't been normal since I met you and you know it."

"True." He chuckled. "It's nice to hear, though."

Lori squeezed his fingers, reveling in the warmth and strength of his touch. "Oh, Jason. What are we going to do?"

"You promised me three days."

"We only have a day and a half left."

"Then keep your promise. Trust me."

Lori made a face at him. "I also had a funny stuffed toy shaped like a buzzard when I was a kid," she told him. "One of my sisters gave it to me as a joke. It had a sign around its neck that said the same thing."

"What?"

Lori scowled. "Trust me."

"It's not fair," Annette grumbled. "We had enough time to play another round. We shouldn't be penalized just because the blue team dudded out."

"Vicki explained all that," Lori said, piloting the Mustang down the freeway toward home. "We'll get our second clue tomorrow."

"Yeah. I know." Pouting, Annette stared out the window for a few seconds, then turned back to Lori, smiling. "Did I tell you about Charlie?"

"The cameraman? Yes. At least six times."

"He likes me."

"So you said. His buddies seemed to like you, too."

Annette grinned. "Yeah. A couple of them are real cute. Especially the one who had to follow that stupid blue team around today."

"They never found their flag?"

Chuckling, Annette said, "Nope. We're ahead. Isn't that wonderful?"

Lori nodded. Wonderful. Assuming you gave a damn about the stupid game. Jason had bid her a terse goodbye with no mention of their spending the evening together. Worse yet, the last time she'd seen him, he'd been standing at the entrance to Affiliated Broadcasting surrounded by

Ruby, Vicki and Simone, seemingly unconcerned that the woman he was supposed to be madly in love with was driving away. Men!

"Do you want to come over to my house while I alter those pants for you?" Lori asked.

"Uh, no. Never mind. I've kind of gotten used to them. Just drop me at home, okay?"

"Okay." Well, that corked it. Lori was destined to spend the evening alone with no one but Muggsy to take her mind off her misbegotten romance. Swell. Almost as much fun as washing her hair.

"I thought you'd be out romancing your teammate," Vicki said. "Why did you want to see us?"

"Because it's time to end the charade," Jason said. He extended his hand to Ruby. "My name is Jason Daniels. I'm the new assistant to Mr. McAlister."

"Oh, Lord!" Politely, Ruby accepted his hand. "I should have known."

"I sincerely hope not. And don't look so scared. You did a fine job."

"The show has logistical problems," Ruby said, lifting the top sheet on her clipboard so he could see the paper beneath it. "I made these notes today."

Vicki leaned over, peering at what she'd written. "You can't shut us down. We have to finish taping. Tomorrow's the last day."

Calmly, Ruby turned and shielded her notes so only Jason could see them. "I overheard this, too," she said, pointing to the paper. "One of our people is going with me tonight to see if anyone shows up." Hesitating, she looked seriously at Jason. "Would you like to come?"

"Yes and no," he said. "The affection I feel for Ms. Kendall is no act, I assure you. Under the circumstances, I think it would be better if I left the problem in your capable hands."

"Agreed."

"And my identity will remain our secret until tomorrow?"

She offered her hand once again. "Of course. My pleasure."

"Then let me see you to your car." Bidding Vicki and Simone good-night, he stuffed his hands into the pockets of his slacks and walked slowly away with Ruby.

"It's too bad," she said.

"What is?"

"You and Ms. Kendall. That's a tough situation. I'm glad it's not me in your shoes. You have my sympathy."

"Thanks. I'm afraid I may need it."

"No question. If you were my lover and I found out what you'd been doing, I'd be furious."

"Lori's very forgiving."

"Why don't you break the news to her tonight?"

"You know why I can't."

"Yeah. Sorry." She brightened. "Tomorrow morning, then? I can hold off making my announcement till you've had a few minutes alone with her."

Jason laid his hand on Ruby's arm. "You'd do that?"

"Sure. It's not breaking any rules."

"I'll be eternally grateful."

"If you pull this off, Mr. Daniels, you'll be more than that. You'll be the luckiest man alive."

"To have Lori?"

"To have lived through one of old man McAlister's tests. He fired the last three men he appointed to your position."

Chapter Ten

But we can't go without Jason," Lori argued, grasping Annette's arm. The night before had been disastrous, and the morning seemed destined to be even worse. If that was possible. Lori scanned the Affiliated Broadcasting parking lot. Still no sign of Jason or the red Ferrari.

Vicki's lips formed a smile that stopped before it reached her eyes. "Mr. Daniels phoned to tell us he'd been detained. It's no problem, really. As soon as he arrives, he'll be escorted to our location and today's contest will begin."

"If he makes us forfeit to the yellow team," Annette hissed, "I'll kill him."

Looking back over her shoulder, Lori started to climb into her team's van. "I don't understand what happened to him." Pausing on the step, she shivered. A cold chill raced through her, despite the day's warmth, and she felt terribly uneasy.

Annette scowled at her. "What's the matter?"

"I don't know. I think I sensed someone watching us."

"Well, you'd better get over worrying about that," Annette warned. "Pretty soon, all of America's going to be watching both of us!"

Lori grimaced. "Please. Don't remind me."

Three stories above the parking lot, Jason stood at a window, looking down and seeing his hope for the future driving away. He turned to pace across the floor. Brad Fox had delivered the summons to McAlister's office and was now waiting with his old friend.

"He did say nine-thirty, didn't he?"

Brad nodded. "Yeah. He made a big deal about promptness, too."

"Lori just left with the *Treasure Hunters* crew."

"Hey, buddy, I'm sorry. I only delivered the message."

"I know." Frowning, Jason stalked back to the window. "Did you hear how it went at the zoo last night?"

"She was there, if that's what you mean. She'd changed clothes and covered up all her fuzzy blond hair, but it was her, all right. No doubt about it."

"And you're sure she was alone?"

"Ruby said so. She also said she's going to pull the plug on your scheming little teammate this morning."

"I know." Jason straightened his tie. "And if I'm not there, chances are I'll never get the chance to explain things adequately to Lori."

He started for the exit, his mind suddenly made up. "Tell McAlister I had another appointment." Jason paused, his hand on the doorknob. "And if he hollers, tell him I quit."

Brad was on his feet in less than a second. "You can't mean that."

"I can and I do. His crazy ideas may have already cost me the love of the woman I intend to spend the rest of my life with. *No* job is worth losing Lori." Hesitating, he glared at Brad. "And you can tell him I said so."

"But . . . you'll never catch them in time."

Jason's jaw was tight, his eyes gleaming with purpose. "Oh, no? Watch me."

He sped into the observatory parking lot expecting to find the same chaotic scene as the day before, but the lot was empty. Coming to a screeching halt, Jason slammed his fist against the steering wheel. Of course. They must have moved their home base to the zoo. That was where today's action was scheduled to take place. Why hadn't he thought of that?

And if they're not there, then what? Jason asked himself. He supposed he could steal a few minutes to phone the studio and ask where *Treasure Hunters* was being taped, but by the time he'd been passed from one person who didn't know to another who probably didn't, either, it would be too late.

Jamming the Ferrari in gear, he roared away from the observatory toward the zoo. The sports car was made for roads like this, he thought, whipping it around the hairpin turns and managing to stay on his side of the double yellow line through most of the corners. Terrain was flying by, but so was time. To make it to the zoo before Ruby dropped the ax on Annette, he'd have to be either a superb driver or a damn lucky son of a gun.

Jason crested the last hill. The objects of his search, three vans and a transport vehicle, were parked in a line. They looked deserted. Accelerating for the final hundred yards, he skidded to a halt behind the Affiliated Broadcasting truck.

Leaping from his car, Jason began to beat on the truck's rear door. It was opened by a man wearing a headset and sipping coffee from a cup. "Hey, buddy. Keep your shirt on."

"Where are they?" Jason demanded.

The man gestured toward the zoo entrance. "The contestants? In there. We're not taping, yet." He stared. "Say, aren't you one of them?"

"Yes." Jason took off running for the gate.

"But you've got to have an escort from Fair Practices. You can't just go running around loose in there. Hey, mister!"

Ignoring everyone and everything, Jason slapped a twenty-dollar bill in the ticket window. "One! And keep the change." He grabbed the orange ticket, threw it at the gateman, and jumped the turnstile.

Which way? *Which way!* There were four possible directions the group could have gone, one for each major continent. One chance in four of guessing right. Lousy odds.

A sailor in crisp whites passed. Jason accosted him. "Have you seen a bunch of people in sweat suits being followed by mobile television cameras?" From the blank look he received, Jason decided not and turned away.

A zookeeper! He'd know what was going on in his territory. Running one hand over his hair to smooth it and calm himself, Jason approached the man. "Hello. I was wondering if you could tell me where they're filming the game show today?"

"Game show? Don't know nothin' about it. We got a seal show this afternoon, though. Bet you'd enjoy that."

"No. No, thanks." Breathing hard, Jason pivoted, scanning the crowd. Who would be likely to have taken notice of cameras and the unusual group of people making up *Treasure Hunters*? Two gray-haired women who looked enough alike to be sisters were peering down at a map, pointing and obviously disagreeing. He straightened his jacket. It was worth a try.

"Excuse me, ladies. I'm from out of town and I heard there was going to be a TV show filmed here today. Have either of you seen any cameras?"

The one on the left tilted up her green plastic visor and squinted at him. "I sure have. Helen here swears it was all in my head and she won't go with me to see."

Jason reached out to grab her by the shoulders, stopping himself just in time. "Where? Which way did they go?"

"Tell Helen I'm not senile."

"No, you're fine." Jason gave in to the irresistible urge to touch her arm. "Please? Which way?"

She pointed toward the path to the African exhibits, breaking into a wide, wrinkled grin when Jason planted a quick kiss on her cheek.

"Thanks!"

"Anytime, young man," she said, shooting an I-told-you-so look at her companion.

Coattails flying, Jason raced off. Breath burned his lungs. He hooked his index finger through his tie and loosened it, then unbuttoned his collar. The muscles in his legs were on fire, his whole body aching. Just a few more yards, he told himself. Don't give up. You'll make it.

Rounding the corner by the lions' grotto, Jason spotted his quarry one level below. All the teams were still together. Vicki had climbed up on a bench and was obviously delivering a speech. *The* speech. It had to be.

He slowed his pace. He might be too far away to see details of facial expressions, but there was no doubt what the contestants were feeling. He could sense their animosity, see it in their body language.

And Lori. What about Lori? Scanning the crowd, he found her. She was standing stiffly, her head held at a proud angle, facing Vicki. If only he could see her expression, read her thoughts, then maybe he could figure out what to say to her.

Breathing raggedly, Jason stopped. What could he tell her that would undo the damage being inflicted this very minute? And what made him think Lori would be in the mood to listen?

* * *

"So that's why he didn't show up this morning," Lori muttered. "His job was done." There was a name for what she was feeling. It went far beyond anger. It was betrayal, above all else. Jason had vowed that he loved her, had made her believe he cared. And now... What a fool she'd been. How he must have laughed at her gullibility.

Tears welled up in Lori's eyes and spilled silently down her cheeks.

"Therefore," Vicki was saying, "in view of the cheating we've uncovered, the red team is disqualified. The yellow team will take its place."

Annette bit her lower lip. "I don't believe this is happening."

"Believe it," Lori said with a quaver in her voice.

"What?" Annette stared. "You knew, didn't you? All that whispering and secret talk was just more spying, wasn't it? He told you all about himself and you didn't think enough of me as a friend to warn me!"

"Oh, stop it." The tears were flowing freely now, and Lori wiped them away with her fingertips. "He didn't tell me a thing."

"Oh, sure. Protect Jason. Go ahead."

Lori's anger rose to the surface. "I'm *not* protecting him. I'm the one he played for a fool. I never want to see him again."

Vicki's voice cut through Lori's fury. "In that case, I'd say you have a problem. It seems our Mr. Daniels has finally arrived."

Spinning to follow Vicki's gaze, Lori saw Jason walking slowly down the hill. As handsome as ever, the sight of him brought a sob to her throat. His real life wasn't anything like she'd imagined it to be, yet her heart was still inexorably drawn to him like the tide to the shore.

She couldn't stand there and face him. Not now. Not when everyone in the group knew how close they'd grown.

Correction. How close Lori had been to him. As for Jason's feelings, he'd proved how little he cared by the shoddy way he'd treated her.

With her pulse thudding in her ears, her head aching and her vision blurred by tears, Lori wasn't sure she could elude him. The only thing she *was* certain of was that she had to try. She turned on her heel, forced her way through the crowd and ran.

Jason saw her go. She was fleeing as if the devil himself was after her.

He tried calling. "Lori! No! Wait!"

It was no use. She only ran more quickly. Plunging down the hill, she rounded a corner and disappeared from view.

Jason moved faster and faster. People tried to stop him and failed as he careered by. He was a man obsessed. Lori was hurting. He had to reach her. Had to take her in his arms. Had to kiss away her tears and explain why he'd remained undercover even after he'd fallen in love with her.

He dashed past the spot where she had disappeared, slowed his pace and scanned the visitors. Lori had to be among them somewhere. A flash of red fabric caught his eye and he was off again. There!

No, there.

Three times he thought he had her and three times he saw he'd made a mistake.

At last, Jason spotted the red sweat suit he was searching for. Thank God she'd stopped running. Breathless and barely coherent, he grabbed her by one shoulder and spun her around.

It wasn't Lori. "I—I'm sorry. I thought . . ."

He released the stranger and pivoted in the midst of the crowd, ignoring the stares he'd garnered by his behavior and frantic appearance. Beads of perspiration stood out on his forehead. Shedding his coat, he slung it over one shoulder and pulled his tie the rest of the way off. He wasn't giving up. If Lori was still in the zoo, he'd find her.

* * *

Lori ran until the ache in her heart was overshadowed by the burning pain in her lungs and the almost incapacitating weakness in her legs. She knew she'd long ago escaped from Jason, yet she continued to run to purge him from her soul.

She didn't care that her mad dash was attracting attention along the way. Nor did she try to hide her tears. Beyond caring, she ran till she couldn't take one more step, then sank to her knees on a grassy knoll between two exhibits and buried her head in her hands.

Of all the secrets Jason could have had, why did it have to be one he could have safely shared with her? Why couldn't he have been a spy for the CIA, or a police officer chasing dangerous drug dealers, or at least involved in something beyond her scope of understanding?

But, no. Jason Daniels—if that was really his name—was doing a job that made perfect sense to her. Lori was in total agreement that someone like Ruby was a necessary part of the game-show staff. Couldn't he see that? Couldn't he have trusted her?

And what about poor Annette? Lori drew a ragged breath, pulled her knees up to her chin and looked out at the peacefully isolated, shady slope. It was still hard to believe Annette had come to the zoo to search for another flag before getting an official clue. It was, however, quite possible that she had picked up information from her interlude with Charlie and the other cameraman. As bent on winning as Annette was, Lori supposed anything was possible. Even cheating.

Lori hurt for her friend's lost dreams, even though it was Annette's improper actions that had led to her disqualification. Jason had been right about that, she conceded. Annette was playing in a competition she took far too seriously for her own good. If it hadn't been Ruby who had exposed her, it would have been someone else.

Closing her eyes and lowering her forehead to her knees, Lori tried to blot out her memories of the past week. "Oh, Jason, why?" she whispered.

Forgetting him was like trying to imagine that the entire universe had disappeared. Dancing in the darkness behind her swollen eyelids was the image of Jason's laughing eyes, his firm mouth, his tall, strong body, his kisses... and his lying tongue.

The futility of his search was slow to penetrate Jason's conscious mind. One more corner, he told himself. One more aisle. She's here. I know she is. I can feel it.

His shirt was soaked with perspiration, his hair disheveled, his suit beyond saving, when he ultimately gave up and started slowly for the parking lot. Once he'd been positive he'd spotted Lori, but the path between exhibits rambled in long, lazy loops and by the time he'd vaulted the locked gates that isolated the maintenance areas and reached the place where he'd seen her, she was gone.

Gone, too, was the last of his hope.

Jason thought seriously of phoning Brad to find out what McAlister's reaction had been to his quitting. Not that it mattered. He swung the Ferrari out into traffic. He'd probably have to give the car back, too, but so what? If he didn't have Lori, what difference did anything make?

There was no place he particularly wanted to go. Out of habit, he followed the 10 freeway to the coast and home.

Lori didn't know where Annette was. It pained her to realize she didn't much care. Annette was as bad as Jason, Lori decided. Neither of them trusted her one bit. Alone in the midst of the milling, happy crowds, Lori dried her tears and made her way toward the exit.

Threads of rational thought were weaving themselves into a pattern of action. She had debts to pay. Oh, yes. She owed Mr. Jason Daniels a scathing lecture he wouldn't soon forget. As for Annette, her punishment had already been meted out, in spades.

Lori passed groups of solicitors waving signs about the end of the world and found their ideas rather apropos. At the curb, she spotted just what she needed, raised her arm, and called, "Taxi!"

The cab dropped her at the gate to Affiliated Broadcasting.

"Hi." Lori greeted the guard, hoping her puffy eyes were somewhat normal in appearance by now. "I got separated from my party and I need to pick up my car." She smiled innocently. "Lori Kendall. Remember?"

"Sure, Ms. Kendall. But the others aren't back yet."

"That's okay. I'll just wander up to the offices and wait."

"Well, I guess that'd be all right." He opened the locked gate. "Go on in."

Lori waved. "Thanks." Obstacle number one overcome, she told herself. Next, a quick stop at her car to pick up her purse and makeup, then on to the offices for the hard part, once she'd camouflaged the ravages caused by her weeping.

Finally satisfied that her reddened eyes couldn't look any better, no matter what she did to them, Lori brazenly pushed open the heavy entry door and entered Affiliated Broadcasting. A security guard was stationed at a console.

"Yes, ma'am. May I help you?"

"I'm here to report to the Fair Practices Department. I have information about the *Treasure Hunters* show." She pinched and pulled at both shoulders of her red sweatshirt to flatten the logo. "See?"

He checked the clipboard. "I don't see any visitors listed for them. Are you sure you're expected?"

"Well, this did come up rather suddenly." Not a lie, Lori reminded herself. Not exactly.

"I see. Maybe I'd better call upstairs. What did you say your name was?"

Uh-oh, Lori thought nervously. If Jason had already passed the word that she was banned, her quest would end in the studio lobby. She supposed she could always throw her planned tantrum right there, but she'd really wanted Jason to get the full benefit of her premier performance.

She swallowed hard. "It's Kendall. Lori Kendall."

The guard dialed, spoke briefly to someone and repeated her name. Twice. "That's right. Okay. I promise."

"Is it okay?" Lori was afraid to hear his answer.

"Oh, yeah. I don't know who you are, lady, but Mr. Fox is on his way down to get you. Made me swear I wouldn't let you out of my sight."

"Terrific." She sank into the overstuffed couch between two enormous potted palms and folded her hands in her lap. So much for launching a surprise attack on Jason Daniels. First, they send a wolf to spy on her and now it's a fox. Funny, Lori. Very funny. You're mad, remember? M-A-D, furious. Hold that thought.

The sandy-haired man who scuttled through the door was so agitated Lori felt instantly sorry for him. On his way to a heart attack before he was fifty if he didn't get a grip on himself, she decided. He extended his hand and grasped hers before she had a chance to offer it.

"Brad Fox," he said. "And you're Lori Kendall."

"Yes, but how—"

"I have all the tests, photos and files," he said. "I must confess, I looked you up."

"Oh."

"How did it go this morning?" Brad scanned her face. "That bad, huh? I figured as much when Jason didn't show up back here." Releasing her hand, he paced to the counter and back. "Ms. Kendall, can you spare a few minutes to come with me?"

Lori frowned. "No. I'm out for blood, Mr. Fox. If the man I know as Jason Daniels isn't here, then I'll be going."

"That's his real name." Brad held out his hand. "Please? There's someone you should meet. If you agree, I'll provide you with Jason's home address and you can still accomplish your original purpose."

"Honest?" She peered at him. "Why would you do that?"

"Personal reasons." He opened the inner door and held it for her. "Are you coming?"

"Why not?" Lori said. "I have nothing more to lose."

"So he quit. Just like that," Brad told Lori as the elevator rose to the third floor. "Mr. McAlister's been fuming all morning, but we've had no word from Jason. I was kind of hoping he'd caught up with you so he'd have at least one good thing to show for his move to California."

"Then he really is from Chicago?"

"Yes. We both are. That's where we met. Jason got me my first job in broadcasting." Brad led the way into the hall and paused with his hand on the knob of a door marked Private. "Ready?"

Lori nodded as the door swung open. The man Brad Fox seemed to fear was seated behind a desk so immense it dwarfed him. His face was stern, his hair stood in tufts above his ears and collar, and his eyebrows were set on prominent ridges that made them resemble great gray caterpillars, stalking each other. The only features not comical about the older man were his penetrating, cold eyes. They bored into Lori like black lasers.

"So, you're the bit of fluff Daniels went off chasing."

"No, sir." Lori's anger was still in the forefront, but its focus was rapidly shifting.

"What do you mean, no?" He glared at Brad. "I thought you told me she was the one."

"I'm Lori Kendall," she interjected. "I'm a person, not a nameless dust devil kicking around under someone's couch."

Instead of the chastisement she'd expected, McAlister chuckled. "I'm beginning to see what made one of my most promising executives tell me he'd quit, rather than give you up."

He got to his feet, offering her his hand. "I'm pleased to make your acquaintance, Ms. Kendall. Now tell me. What do we have to do to get Daniels back into my department?"

"You want him back?"

McAlister laughed again, his amusement jiggling all three of his chins. "I do. And I daresay you do, too." He patted her hand while shaking it. "There are very few men left in this world who place love and loyalty above monetary gains. I can't afford to let one of them get away." He peered at Lori while the furry caterpillars of his eyebrows wriggled. "Can you?"

"I hadn't given it much thought."

"Bah. You can do better than that."

She found herself chuckling. "Do you always speak your mind like this?"

"Usually. I highly recommend it to my staff."

"Do they stay long?"

"The ones who fit in do." He reached down and picked up a manila folder from his desk. "Your sociological and psychological profile is most impressive."

"You have that, too? I thought it was just for the game show." Lori glanced at Brad, who was doing an excellent imitation of the invisible man. She sobered. "I suppose Jason saw it, too?"

"Of course."

"That hardly seems fair. He knew all about me and he wouldn't even tell me where he lived." Lori turned to Brad. "Which reminds me..."

McAlister's voice grew kinder. "When you've been exposed to more of our ways you'll understand, Ms. Kendall. If Daniels had told you about his undercover assignment he would have jeopardized his entire career, not to mention undermining the excellent work of the rest of our staff. It's a group effort. No one can do it entirely alone.''

"Then why—"

"Why did he quit?" The old man sat down heavily in his chair. "I'm afraid I pushed him into it. And now I'm asking—no, begging—you to help me convince him to come back to work for me."

"Suppose he doesn't want to?"

"This is what he does, Ms. Kendall. It's the career he's followed for most of his adult life. It's not the *job* he hates, it's what he had to do to you that finally made him chuck it all."

"I wish I could believe you." Lori stared blankly out the window.

"It's not me you need to believe, my dear. It's Jason."

Shaking her head, she took a deep breath. "I honestly don't know if I can."

It would have been faster to drive directly to Santa Monica, but Lori needed more time to sort out her thoughts, so she decided to go home first. Besides, if she was going to confront Jason, she wanted to have the advantage of looking her best. He'd paid special attention to her turquoise silk dress, so she chose to don it again.

Muggsy danced at her feet.

"I suppose you think I should make up with him, too, don't you?" she asked the little dog. "Sure. You like him because he feeds you Chinese food."

Memories of their good times came flooding back to Lori. She recalled Jason's sweetly sensual smile and how good it had felt when he'd looked at her with his laughing eyes. Whatever the outcome of their relationship, she knew she'd never forget him. Nor did she want to try.

Reaching for the bag of dog food, Lori filled Muggsy's
bowl and checked to make sure he had enough water. She
ruffled his fuzzy ears. "Don't wait up for me, okay?"

The plumed tail wagged in happy agreement.

All the way to the beach, Lori rehearsed witty speeches
and snappy retorts. By the time she reached Jason's condo
she'd played out her fantasies and used up most of her
stored anger. There was a hole in her life big enough to fly
a 747 through and she knew it.

Jason's address brought her to an exclusive, guarded
condominium complex set behind locked gates and sophisticated alarm systems. Lori pulled to the curb and looked
through the wrought iron bars at the ultraperfect commu-
nity within. It might be all right for some folks, but it looked
like a prison to her. Unsure that she really wanted to storm
those bastions to get to Jason, she hesitated.

The ocean beckoned, offering solace and sweet memories of Jason's kisses. Some of their happiest times had been
spent on the pier and the sand below. Leaving her car, Lori
crossed the street and walked slowly, thoughtfully, toward
the shore.

She climbed the stairs, making her way along the aged
wooden planking. Ocean breezes lifted her hair away from
her face, the tangy salt smells providing the final link between the present and Lori's heartrending remembrances of
Jason.

Pausing at the railing, she looked down at the waves
crashing against the barnacle-encrusted pilings. Water swept
across the sand in hypnotic repetitions, lulling her senses and
bringing a true realization of what she might be throwing
away if she let her pride keep her from listening to Jason's
explanations.

Jason Daniels might not be perfect, but neither was she.
It had to be better to take a chance on love than to let it slip

through her fingers and never know what she'd missed; what she'd carelessly thrown away.

Lori felt a catch in her throat and her pulse began to race. Below, walking along the sand, was a man whose posture gave the impression of utter dejection. His hands were stuffed in the pockets of his slacks, his usually broad shoulders were slumped and he was kicking at imaginary objects in the sand beneath his feet.

She leaned over to get a better look, knowing before he turned to face her that it was Jason. The self-assurance had gone out of him. He was hurting, too, and he needed her. Lori's heart opened and she set aside all her own anguish, real or imagined, in that one instant of unconditional love.

Without a moment's pause she called down, "Hey, mister."

Jason looked up and saw her waving.

"Mister! Wanna have some fun?"

Jason's face changed before her eyes. Gone were the worry lines and the suffering. He stood straighter. He smiled. "Hello."

"I'm all dressed up. Want to buy me another shrimp cocktail?"

Extending his arms and holding out his palms, he gestured wildly. "Stay there! Don't move! I'll be right up."

Lori couldn't wait. She started back down the pier as Jason ran along the sand below her. He leaped up the stairs two at a time, reaching the top at the same instant she did.

Only a few feet separated them. Lori hesitated, still unsure.

Jason opened his arms to her. "I love you, Lori."

In an instant she was in his embrace, holding him close and promising herself she'd never let him go as long as she lived. "I love you, too." She felt him draw a ragged breath, then bury his face in her hair.

"Oh, honey. I thought I'd lost you."

"You almost did," Lori said softly. She leaned back to look into his eyes, not at all surprised to find her tears of joy mirrored there. "We have a lot of catching up to do. You owe me some explanations, mister."

Lifting her off the ground, Jason swung her around in exuberant circles. "Anything you say." He kissed her adoringly. "As long as we're together."

"Well, I suppose we could begin by seeing your home." Lori giggled. "Do you have any etchings?"

"I'll buy some." Jason caught her around the waist and pulled her against his side as they walked. "In the meantime, you're stuck with listening to the story of my life."

Lori found Jason's condo impressive. The best thing about it, of course, was the fact that *he* lived there. She'd removed her shoes and was lying on the soft cushions of the modern white couch with her head resting in Jason's lap. He stroked her hair as he finished telling her about his move to California and the surprises his new boss had had in store for him.

"I have a current résumé," Jason said, "and I'll start making the rounds with it tomorrow." He glanced up at the milky walls and sea-foam-green accents of his apartment. "Don't get too attached to this place. It was one of the perks from Affiliated."

"Don't worry. It's not my style, anyway." Lori rolled onto her side and smiled up at him. "Which reminds me, I have a message for you from a funny-looking little man with more hair on his eyebrows than he has on his head."

"McAlister? When did you talk to him?"

"This morning. He called me a 'bit of fluff' and I let him have it."

Jason chuckled. "Good for you. If I hadn't been in such a hurry to catch up to you, I'd have done the same thing."

"So I gathered." She tucked her legs under her and sat up. "The odd thing is, the man wants you back."

"To feed to the sharks, I suppose."

"I don't think so. He seemed sincere. Says men who put love and loyalty first are rare."

"He said that?"

Lori nodded. "And I agree. You did what you had to do. I wish you'd confided in me, but..."

He cradled her face in his hands, stroking her cheeks and tucking her hair behind her ears. "Don't you see, honey? I couldn't. You'd have had to lie, either to me or to your friends if I'd told you who I really was."

A broad smile lifted the corners of Jason's mouth, making his eyes twinkle with delight and desire. "And you, my love, are the worst liar on the face of the earth."

"Thanks, I think." Lori placed her hands on his shoulders, letting her fingers tease the hairs on the back of his neck. "Can I ask you something personal?"

"Anything." His heart was pounding from her nearness and he would gladly have divulged any and all of his deepest, darkest secrets. Whatever Lori wanted from him was hers.

She looked at him seriously. "On the psychological part of the test, was I supposed to find the old man with the dog a new apartment?"

Jason's warm laugh filled the room. "Yes, Lori. That was the only way to solve the problem without hurting anyone or breaking any rules. I knew you'd choose that solution."

"Good." Her smile was self-satisfied.

"Now, do I get to ask you a personal question?"

"But you already know all about me."

"Not all." Jason's voice vibrated softly as he pulled her across his lap and cradled her in his arms. "I don't know yet if you'll agree to marry me."

She could scarcely speak. "No more secrets?"

"Not from each other," Jason promised. "And I'll find another profession if my job bothers you."

She moved closer. "I'm proud of you and of what you do. I'll be the proudest wife at the company picnics."

Kissing her forehead, Jason smiled down on her. "I don't think Affiliated Broadcasting has company picnics."

"Not yet. But you wait and see. McAlister owes me a favor and I think your department could use a morale boost. Brad Fox certainly could."

"He'll be the best man."

"In our wedding party, maybe," Lori said. "But as far as I'm concerned, the best man is right here beside me."

"And you never lie." Jason stood and lifted her into his arms. "Would you like to go upstairs and discuss our wedding before I go crazy wanting you?"

"Yes, oh, yes," Lori whispered. "And I *never* lie."

* * * * *

COMING NEXT MONTH

#658 A WOMAN IN LOVE—Brittany Young
When archaeologist Melina Chase met the mysterious Aristo
Drapano aboard a treasure-hunting ship in the Greek isles, she
knew he was her most priceless find....

#659 WALTZ WITH THE FLOWERS—Marcine Smith
When Estella Blaine applied for a loan to build a stable on her
farm, she never expected bank manager Cody Marlowe to ask for
her heart as collateral!

#660 IT HAPPENED ONE MORNING—Jill Castle
A chance encounter in the park with free-spirited dog trainer
Collier Woolery had Neysa Williston's orderly heart spinning.
Could he convince her that their meeting was destiny?

#661 DREAM OF A LIFETIME—Arlene James
Businessman Dan Wilson needed an adventure and found one in
the Montana Rockies with lovely mountain guide Laney Scott.
But now he wanted her to follow his trail....

#662 THE WEDDING MARCH—Terry Essig
Feisty five-foot Lucia Callahan had had just about enough of
tall, protective men, and she set out to find a husband her own
size...but she couldn't resist Daniel Statler—all six feet of him!

#663 NO WAY TO TREAT A LADY—Rita Rainville
Aunt Tillie was at it again, matchmaking between her llama-
ranching nephew, Dave McGraw, and reading teacher Jennifer
Hale. True love would never be the same again!

AVAILABLE THIS MONTH:

#652 THE ENCHANTED SUMMER
Victoria Glenn

**#653 AGELESS PASSION,
TIMELESS LOVE**
Phyllis Halldorson

#654 HIS KIND OF WOMAN
Pat Tracy

#655 TREASURE HUNTERS
Val Whisenand

#656 IT TAKES TWO
Joan Smith

#657 TEACH ME
Stella Bagwell

FOUR UNIQUE SERIES
FOR EVERY WOMAN YOU ARE...

Silhouette Romance

Love, at its most tender, provocative, emotional... in stories that will make you laugh and cry while bringing you the magic of falling in love.

6 titles per month

Silhouette Special Edition

Sophisticated, substantial and packed with emotion, these powerful novels of life and love will capture your imagination and steal your heart.

6 titles per month

Silhouette Desire

Open the door to romance and passion. Humorous, emotional, compelling—yet always a believable and sensuous story—Silhouette Desire never fails to deliver on the promise of love.

6 titles per month

Silhouette Intimate Moments

Enter a world of excitement, of romance heightened by suspense, adventure and the passions every woman dreams of. Let us sweep you away.

4 titles per month

SILG-1R

"GIVE YOUR HEART TO SILHOUETTE" SWEEPSTAKES
OFFICIAL RULES
NO PURCHASE NECESSARY TO ENTER OR RECEIVE A PRIZE

1. To enter and join the Silhouette Reader Service, rub off the concealment device on all game tickets. This will reveal the potential value for each Sweepstakes entry number and the number of free book(s) you will receive. Accepting the free book(s) will automatically entitle you to also receive a free bonus gift. If you do not wish to take advantage of our introduction to the Silhouette Reader Service but wish to enter the Sweepstakes only, rub off the concealment device on tickets #1-3 only. To enter, return your entire sheet of tickets. Incomplete and/or inaccurate entries are not eligible for that section or section (s) of prizes. Not responsible for mutilated or unreadable entries or inadvertent printing errors. Mechanically reproduced entries are null and void.

2. Either way, your Sweepstakes numbers will be compared against the list of winning numbers generated at random by computer. In the event that all prizes are not claimed, random drawings will be made from all entries received from all presentations to award all unclaimed prizes. All cash prizes are payable in U.S. funds. This is in addition to any free, surprise or mystery gifts that might be offered. The following prizes are awarded in this sweepstakes:

(1)	*Grand Prize	$1,000,000	Annuity
(1)	First Prize	$35,000	
(1)	Second Prize	$10,000	
(3)	Third Prize	$5,000	
(10)	Fourth Prize	$1,000	
(25)	Fifth Prize	$500	
(5000)	Sixth Prize	$5	

*The Grand Prize is payable through a $1,000,000 annuity. Winner may elect to receive $25,000 a year for 40 years, totaling up to $1,000,000 without interest, or $350,000 in one cash payment. Winners selected will receive the prizes offered in the Sweepstakes promotion they receive.
Entrants may cancel the Reader Service privileges at any time without cost or obligation to buy (see details in center insert card).

3. Versions of this Sweepstakes with different graphics may be offered in other mailings or at retail outlets by Torstar Corp. and its affiliates. This promotion is being conducted under the supervision of Marden-Kane, Inc., an independent judging organization. By entering this Sweepstakes, each entrant accepts and agrees to be bound by these rules and the decisions of the judges, which shall be final and binding. Odds of winning are dependent upon the total number of entries received. Taxes, if any, are the sole responsibility of the winners. Prizes are nontransferable. All entries must be received by March 31, 1990. The drawing will take place on April 30, 1990, at the offices of Marden-Kane, Inc., Lake Success, N.Y.

4. This offer is open to residents of the U.S., Great Britain and Canada, 18 years or older, except employees of Torstar Corp., its affiliates, and subsidiaries, Marden-Kane, Inc. and all other agencies and persons connected with conducting this Sweepstakes. All federal, state and local laws apply. Void wherever prohibited or restricted by law.

5. Winners will be notified by mail and may be required to execute an affidavit of eligibility and release that must be returned within 14 days after notification. Canadian winners will be required to answer a skill-testing question. Winners consent to the use of their name, photograph and/or likeness for advertising and publicity in conjunction with this and similar promotions without additional compensation. One prize per family or household.

6. For a list of our most current major prizewinners, send a stamped, self-addressed envelope to: WINNERS LIST, c/o MARDEN-KANE, INC., P.O. BOX 701, SAYREVILLE, N.J. 08871

If Sweepstakes entry form is missing, please print your name and address on a 3"×5" piece of plain paper and send to:

In the U.S.	In Canada
Sweepstakes Entry	Sweepstakes Entry
901 Fuhrmann Blvd.	P.O. Box 609
P.O. Box 1867	Fort Erie, Ontario
Buffalo, NY 14269-1867	L2A 5X3

LTY-S69R